ANTIDOTE:

Love and War, Book 1

R. A. STEFFAN

Antidote: Love and War, Book 1

Copyright 2017 by R. A. Steffan

This book is a work of fiction. Names, characters, businesses, organizations, places, events and incidents either are the product of the author's imagination or are used fictitiously. Any resemblance to actual persons, living or dead, events, or locales is entirely coincidental.

ISBN: 978-1-955073-48-6 (paperback)

For information, contact the author at
http://www.rasteffan.com/contact/

Cover design by Ember

Second Edition: July 2022

INTRODUCTION

This book contains graphic violence and explicit sexual content. It is intended for a mature audience. While it is part of a series with an overarching plot, it can be read as a standalone with a happy ending for the two main characters, and a satisfying resolution of the storyline.

TABLE OF CONTENTS

ONE

If I die now, everyone back home dies with me. I can't die now.

"Oh, gods, *I can't die now.*" The words were barely audible over the shriek of a space vessel pushed to its limit and beyond.

Skye Chantrell was not normally a religious woman, but there was something about the sight of a planet's surface rushing far too quickly toward the cracked viewport of her stolen, rusted-out shuttle that brought the old superstitions flooding back.

Please, please, please, she prayed. *Not now, not here, not like this!*

When she'd fled the Regime's complex at the border of the demilitarized zone, she'd barely managed to escape with her life. If the shuttle she'd taken hadn't already been damaged and leaking fuel when she entered the wormhole gate at the edge of the system, her pursuers would have tracked her down and finished the job in no time at all. As it was, the craft's malfunctioning engines had flung her randomly through the vortex before spitting her out here, in the gravitational well of an old, abandoned outpost on some unremarked, forgotten moon.

With no other options available, she ran through the emergency restart procedure one last time. Her breath locked in her throat as the aging thrusters coughed, sputtered, and fired weakly into life. She was thrown forward, hard, against her seat restraints as the engines tried to slow the descent, but she could tell it wasn't… going… to be… enough…

Her father had entrusted her with the most important data file in the Seven Systems, at the cost of his own life. She hadn't even had a chance to mourn him yet, and now she was going to join him.

She had failed, and that failure meant a death toll on a scale she could barely imagine. Her hands slid from the controls and fell to her sides.

"I'm so sorry, Daddy," she whispered, as the ground raced up to meet her.

◆

The alarm blared through the old lunar outpost, shrill and jarring. Hunter jerked his head up from the holographic star map he and Kade had been examining, meeting the other Vithii male's cold gray eyes with a frown.

"Perimeter breach," Kade said unnecessarily. The two of them moved toward the door as one, jogging side-by-side through a warren of dingy gray corridors toward the control room.

Hunter already had his comm unit out as they ran, and was barking into it. "Draven! What have we got?"

"Ilarian shuttle," came the static-riddled reply. "Looks like Regime registration, but it's outdated. They don't use these codes anymore. It's coming in hot—crash-landing trajectory. Engines are inactive."

"Where?" Hunter snapped.

"About half a klick north of us," Draven reported. "Just west of the big crater."

They were nearly to the control room. "Right," Hunter said. "Kade and I will be with you in a moment. Stand by."

Kade's voice was grim. "This could be bad."

"Or it could be nothing," Hunter countered. "It all depends on who else—if anyone—is following along behind our unlucky shuttle pilot."

The only reply was a skeptical grunt.

Hunter slid to a stop in front of the heavy durasteel door and slapped his palm to the reader. The slab of metal screeched open on ancient tracks, exposing the simple control center beyond. Draven was alone, his massive, hard-muscled frame bent over the sensor interface. He glanced up as they entered, gold eyes glittering beneath his head of spiky copper-colored hair, then looked right back down again, intent on the screen before him.

"Kill that klaxon," Hunter said. "I think we've all got the point by now. Is the shuttle down yet?"

Draven fumbled for the override without looking, and the shrieking alarm cut off. "Looks like the pilot managed to get the thrusters firing on emergency power. It's veering southeast, closer to us."

There was a low rumble, vibrating the deck plates under their boots. "That was it. It's down," Draven reported.

The door screeched open again, admitting Ryder and Pax. Pax immediately crossed to join Draven at the controls; his metallic facial implants glinting in the blue light of the readouts.

Ryder—a strongly built Vithii woman with a head full of spiky red hair—turned to Kade and

Hunter instead. "What the fuck was that?" she asked. "Meteor strike?"

Kade snorted. "Yeah, right. We should be so lucky."

Hunter—who preferred to leave most of the sarcasm to Kade, who had a flair for it—filled Ryder in quickly on what they knew.

She frowned. "I don't much like the idea that someone could have just randomly crashed on our doorstep. There's no sign of other vessels approaching?"

"Not so far," Draven said. "Looks like your standard engine malfunction. Which is not to say that no one was after them. I don't know about you, but when I see a rusted out piece of junk with bad ID codes, I think *stolen*."

Kade raised a dark, sardonic brow. "Maybe they came to the right place after all, in that case. Assuming they're not charred meat now, of course."

Hunter brought his focus back to the matter at hand. "Life signs?"

"Weak," Draven reported. "Human. Just one, looks like."

Hunter's brow furrowed. What was a human doing with a possibly stolen Regime shuttle, way out here in the badlands? "What's the craft's condition?"

Pax answered, the slight robotic rasp of his implants giving his voice a flat, mechanical dimension. "Engines are burned out. Life support fading quickly. Multiple cabin leaks. It'll lose atmosphere before long."

"Better decide what you want to do here, Hunter," Ryder told him. "Or the problem's going to be a self-limiting one."

While there was something to be said for letting this possible witness to their whereabouts expire quietly in the wreckage, there was also something to be said for finding out who they were, what they were doing here, and—perhaps most importantly—who, if anyone, was likely to be coming after them.

As was often the case, Kade's mind was traveling on a parallel course to his. "Of course, the smart thing to do would be to let the pilot die and vaporize the evidence that anyone was ever here," Kade said. "The less smart thing would be to drag them back here to the base, patch them up, and question them." His flat gaze rested on Hunter for a long moment. "So I'll just go set up the medbay, I guess, since I assume you'll want Ryder to go out there with you."

Ryder's lips twisted in displeasure, but she only said, "Let me go grab a kit. I'll meet you at the airlock. Pax? I may need you when we get back, depending on how bad it is."

Pax nodded—a single, precise movement of acknowledgement. Hunter left without another word, heading to the airlock to check the environmental suits. Ryder was their medic, and a damned good one, for all that she hated having those skills called on. Little wonder, given her past—but the fact remained that when someone needed to be put back together, she was the one to do it.

This particular search and retrieval mission would be complicated by the lack of an atmosphere on the tiny moon. At least the low gravity outside of the artificially generated field within the compound would let them move faster.

6

The e-suits in the locker next to the main air-lock were old, but they were also carefully and regularly serviced. Hunter pulled out his and Ryder's and started safety checks, inspecting the seals and venting the air tanks to confirm the system pressure. A moment later, Ryder came jogging down the corridor, med-pac in hand.

"Dunno what we're likely to find," she warned. "There may not be much I can do."

Hunter shrugged. "Then you'll make Kade happy. Win-win."

She scoffed. "Kade? Happy? You're bent. You must've been at his stash or something."

Hunter didn't bother to point out that anyone stupid enough to raid Kade's stash of neurotonin stabilizers wouldn't still be upright and using both legs afterward. Instead, he helped her suit up, and she did the same for him. He grabbed a portable sensor padd and the human-sized environmental suit they kept on hand for Ash to use when he was here. When he had everything he thought they'd need, he followed her into the airlock, where they waited for the air to cycle.

The outer hatch rolled open and they stepped out onto the moon's barren surface, steadying themselves across the gravity gradient. Hunter spun slowly on the spot, the sensor padd held in front of him. When the directional map lit with an orange star indicating the crash site, he pointed and led the way, falling into the long, efficient, low-grav hops that carried him quickly across the dusty gray landscape—confident that Ryder was right behind him.

⸺◆⸺

The crash site was a mess. Of course, it could have been worse—one of the few saving graces of these old *Dorish*-class shuttles was that the cabins had been built like assault tanks.

The thing had come in low, plowing a furrow with its square belly rather than nose-diving straight into oblivion. Pretty much every extraneous piece of it had been deposited along the way in a trail of crumpled metal that stretched easily for a quarter-klick. Hunter supposed they'd been lucky that it hadn't smashed into the compound directly. In the grand scheme of things, it had come uncomfortably close to them.

Which once again raised the question of whether this whole scenario was a coincidence, or whether someone knew to come nosing around this particular lunar outpost, looking for them. Hopefully, there would be enough left of the pilot to give them some answers.

The ugly, angular central mass of the downed ship was slowly venting atmosphere from a number of leaks, but the airlock was accessible and didn't look too badly damaged. He and Ryder approached cautiously, but the sensor padd confirmed only a single life sign inside, badly injured. Hardly a threat to two Vithii, given how much stronger they were than even a healthy human.

They tested the airlock controls, but the system was dead. Hunter pulled a battery pack lead from his suit and plugged it into the controls, cursing as his heavy gloves made the movement clumsy and slow. After the few moments it took to power up, the outer door shrieked open halfway and stuck.

He unplugged the battery lead, and they slid through the gap. After a repeat of the process on the other side, the door reluctantly screeched shut again. There was no way the failing systems would be able to pump air into the lock to equalize it, so they immediately set to work on the inner door.

With a thin whistle of wind as air from the cabin rushed in to fill the airlock, the inner door slid open, revealing a dark interior lit only by the intermittent sparking of damaged electronics. They both switched on helmet lights, the beams cutting jagged, sodium-yellow swathes through the smoky cabin.

The airlock was aft; the pilot's seat was fore. A slender figure lay face down across the sputtering control panel like a broken doll. Human, as the sensors had said. Female, with long blond hair half-covering the face, matted in places with that startlingly red human blood that never looked quite real to Hunter, even after all this time.

Ryder was already unsealing and pulling off her suit gloves, rummaging in the med-pac for a scanner. Hunter stayed back, fighting down the hot rush of painful memory that seeing a badly injured human woman always raised in him. It was a reaction he could have lived without, but he knew all too well that scars laid down in childhood never healed quite right, whether they were physical or mental. It took only a moment to push the unwanted images from the past back where they belonged, and then he stepped forward to join the reluctant medic.

"Concussion, spinal trauma, five broken ribs, multiple breaks in the arms and legs…" Ryder recited, as if to herself. She paused to glare at the med sensor and give it a shake. "Fucking human anatomy, how does any self-respecting species manage to evolve kidneys without some kind of protection—"

"Ryder," Hunter prompted.

She grumbled something under her breath and continued. "Internal bleeding, oxygen levels falling fast. Let me get everything splinted up as best I can and we'll make a run for the base. Comm ahead, will you? Tell Pax I'll need to requisition some of his bots for this patch job."

He nodded sharply and toggled his suit's comm unit so he could relay the message. Meanwhile, Ryder efficiently encased the injured pilot's broken limbs in kwick-sleeves to hold them rigid, the thin cylinders inflating instantly to mold to the body's contours and stabilize the fractures.

After she had applied a compact forcefield generator around the woman's neck and torso to minimize further spinal damage during transport, she administered a pressure injection directly to the main artery beneath the jaw.

"Oxygen booster," she explained. "It won't work forever, though. Help me get her into that extra e-suit and let's go. She doesn't have long."

Fortunately, though it was sized for a human, Ash's suit was still huge on her. That made it easier to manhandle her into it while trying not to exacerbate her many injuries more than was necessary.

Hunter studied her silently as he and Ryder worked, trying to figure her out. She was wearing civvies—a sleek black jumpsuit with cargo pockets on the sides of the trousers and a form-fitting sleeveless top. Her face—slack in unconsciousness—was strong-featured, with full lips and sharp cheekbones. A small crystal earring glinted in the lobe of her right ear, and a fine gold chain hung around her neck. Her obvious beauty was marred by a broken nose and swelling all down the right side of her face, already turning to dark bruising. Again, Hunter's gut churned, memories swirling together with Vithii male protective instincts in a muddle of distracting urges that he definitely did *not* need to be dealing with right now. He clenched his jaw and quashed the feeling ruthlessly.

She was not dressed for space travel. And even with the damage inside the shuttle's cabin, it was obvious that the ship had been practically derelict. Hunter was surprised it had flown at all. What was she even *doing* out here?

Finally, Ryder eased the suit's helmet over the human woman's head and checked the seals. "Right. We're good to go. Let's move." Her face twisted in irritation, lit oddly by her helmet's internal illumination. "Shit. We should have brought a stretcher. I've been hanging around the rest of you too long. I must be going soft in the head."

"We'll manage," Hunter said. It wasn't ideal, but with the forcefield stabilizing her spine and the splints holding the broken bones steady, he would simply carry her. Ryder helped him scoop her up and position her in the way that was least likely to do more damage.

Her weight would have been nothing to him even in standard gravity. In the moon's feeble point-six-five gees, it was like holding air. Ryder strode across to jump-start the power systems controlling the outer door. Hunter sheltered the injured woman with his body as the remaining atmosphere inside the shuttle whooshed through the opening in a blast of wind.

Carefully, they maneuvered her unresponsive form through the gap of the bent portal, and headed back to the compound. Hunter covered the distance with long, shallow leaps, absorbing the impact with his knees to avoid jolting the woman in his arms.

They arrived to find Pax waiting in the medbay as promised. His massive arms were crossed, and he regarded the human with his usual impassive expression. Ryder directed Hunter to lay his burden on her less-injured side on the exam table. After setting aside her helmet and gauntlets, she went to get a protoplaser to cut off her patient's environmental suit and clothing.

"Ash is going to blow a gasket when he finds out you sliced the only human-sized e-suit we have to ribbons," Hunter observed.

Ryder shot him a deeply unimpressed look before returning to her work. "Kade can buy him a new one," she said. "Now get out of my hair. I'll let you know if she makes it. In return, you let *us* know if a fleet of Regime goons shows up looking for her. Preferably before we're all vaped."

With a nod to Ryder and a tip of his chin to Pax, Hunter made himself scarce and headed back to the control center to update Kade and Draven. He studiously ignored the way the memory of the human woman's battered face kept rising to the surface of his thoughts.

That kind of sentimental shit was the *last* thing he needed.

TWO

Skye surfaced by degrees from one of those dreams of falling endlessly—panic stretching until it seemed impossible for it to go on any longer. Her body jerked hard, coming fully awake, heart pounding a staccato rhythm against the wall of her chest.

She tried to bolt into a sitting position, but her muscles were strangely weak. An invisible pressure held her in place, preventing even the smallest movement, and a new burst of adrenaline flooded her body.

What the hell?

She tried again to move her hand… to wriggle her feet… to lift her head…

Nothing. Her breathing grew harsh with raw, instinctive terror at being trapped, and the distant beeping sound that had tickled the edges of her awareness ratcheted up another notch. Where was she? What was happening?

It was dark—not pitch black, but dim, like a room with heavy shades drawn. She was lying on something unforgiving. Not hard like metal, but definitely not a proper bed or a mattress. The sound of tech filled the room around her. Not just the fast, rhythmic beeping that seemed to stab at her ears, but also a sort of constant low hum, like you sometimes got with the life support systems in a spaceship or a shuttle.

Her mind stumbled over the thought and seized up completely.

A shuttle.

Gods and prophets. The *shuttle*. The wormhole gate.

The ground, rushing up to meet her. Was she… paralyzed? Dead? Was the afterlife a dim room where you lay alone on a hard table, unable to move? Where was… where was her father?

Another memory surfaced, playing silently, like the old Earth films from history class when she was a kid. Her father, spinning in place under the force of the blaster beam that tore a smoking hole out of his chest and stomach, his body crumpling to the ground in slow motion.

Blind panic surged and dragged her under. The shrill beeping sped up until it was almost a continuous tone. She fought with rabid, animal intensity against the strange force holding her immobile, her mouth open in a silent scream.

There was a sudden commotion next to her, though she couldn't even turn her head enough to see. Something cold pressed against her neck with a stinging hiss.

"Five minutes," said a gruff, female voice, irritation weaving through the words. "I can't even take five minutes to go to the lav for a piss. You'd better be worth it, girl, that's all I can say."

Skye tried to struggle. Tried to drag enough air into her lungs to give voice to her terror. But within seconds, gray fog swirled across her vision and she was back in the dream, falling endlessly.

The next time she regained awareness was a little better. Her arms flailed, grasping for purchase in the darkness, her movements still weak and unco-ordinated. She tried to sit up, only making it partway before falling back. Her lower body was still stuck, and her stomach muscles felt like rubber.

The shrill beeping stabbed her ears again, but this time she was able to identify the sound as a pulse monitor.

"Where—" she gasped. "Where am—" Her voice was a croak. It caught on the second word and she descended into coughing.

"Don't try to move," said a deep, accented voice from the shadows at the edge of the dark-ened room. "Lights, twenty percent."

Ancient strip lighting sputtered into life over-head, pushing the shadows back enough for Skye to see the hulking figure lounging in the corner with crossed arms, the tall, broad body radiating easy grace.

Her first thought was *Vithii*.

Her second thought was, *Oh, shit, they caught me. They caught me. I'm as good as dead*.

When the figure pushed away from the wall and crossed the short distance to the bare medical cot where she was lying, the dim lights played over a riot of tattoos running up the length of his hard-muscled arms. They disappeared under the short sleeves of his form-fitting black shirt, only to reap-pear above the neckline—black feathers, swept and ruffled as if in flight. His features were hard. Cold. Brutal.

Familiar, from a hundred grainy surveillance photos on a hundred vidcasts over the past few years.

Holy prophets.

She hadn't been captured by Regime soldiers. It was worse than that. Instead, she'd somehow managed to stumble into the hands of The Rook—the most feared and hated criminal in the whole of the Seven Systems.

And the gods only knew what he was going to do to her before he killed her.

———◆———

Hunter watched as recognition slid over the human female's face, followed closely by terror. Her pupils grew huge inside the summer-blue rings of her irises, and her rasping breath grew labored as she tried to drag recycled air down her dry throat. Her chest heaved under the plain medbay gown Ryder had dressed her in earlier as a nod to modesty.

Vithii in general had a dim view of humans' bravery, and considered them frightened prey animals who froze or bolted at the first sign of danger. Hunter knew this to be a belief instilled and reinforced largely by Regime propaganda. His own experience had shown him quite a different side to the upstart species that had shared the colony on Ilarius with his own people for more than a century.

Which led him to wonder yet again about the human on the medical table in front of him. She was not reacting like a soldier or a field agent, or even a spy. She was reacting like a civvy who had lapped up every horror story the government-sponsored news media had ever dished out about him—because there was no question that she knew who he was.

As far as she was concerned, that meant he was a murderer, rapist, and torturer who probably ate babies on his days off. However, it did nothing whatsoever to answer his questions about who *she* was and what she was doing here.

He gestured with his chin toward the container of water resting on the tray table next to the cot. "Drink something," he said. "You'll need it so you can answer my questions."

Her eyes were darting around her immediate surroundings now, as if looking for a weapon or means of escape.

"Don't bother," he said. "There's still a forcefield immobilizing your lower body. You're not going anywhere."

Just then, the medbay door slid open, admitting Ryder.

"She awake properly this time?" asked the medic.

Hunter grunted, aware that Ryder could see for herself. The human's gaze flickered to her, still fearful, though perhaps not quite as panicked as she'd been when she was alone with him.

After inclining the head of the cot to support the woman's upper body in a more upright position, Ryder brusquely picked up the water and positioned it so the straw was at her patient's lips.

"Drink," she said in a no-nonsense voice, "or I'll insert a stomach tube and get fluids into you that way."

The woman hesitantly wrapped her lips around the straw and sucked, her huge, frightened eyes flicking back and forth between Hunter and Ryder.

Hunter was considering the most efficient way to begin questioning her without frightening her into a dead faint when the proximity alarm screeched into life for the second time in the space of two short orbital rotations. The human flinched at the sudden noise, jerking back from the water bottle.

"What's that?" she asked, her voice restored enough that it didn't crack on the words.

"*Again*? You have got to be kidding me," Ryder said under her breath.

Hunter's mouth pressed into a grim line. "Stay here," he ordered the medic. "I'll go see what's on our doorstep this time, and comm you if you're needed."

Ryder shook her head in disgust and shrugged a shoulder. "Go on, then. You know where to find me."

Hunter turned his back on the disgruntled Vithii woman and the slender human with long golden hair and frightened blue eyes. He ran down the familiar corridors, activating his comm unit as he went.

Making a habit of this, he thought, and snapped, "Report. Who's up there right now?"

"Kade," came the tinny response. "Pax is with me. Draven's on his way. We've got an unfamiliar ship entering orbit, but it's transmitting Ash's codes. I haven't responded, but it's obvious whoever it is knows we're here. They're hailing us directly."

The door to the control room slid open reluctantly, and Hunter heard the final few words in stereo as Kade turned around to look at him.

"Go ahead and reply," Hunter decided. "No visual. Use voice distortion on our end."

"Shoulda let me install those defensive laser systems we talked about," Pax grumbled from his perch against the console next to the communications relay.

"Figure out a way to mask the energy signature from long-range scanners and I will," Hunter shot back, weary of the longstanding argument. "Weapons won't do much good if having them here lights up the whole moon like a beacon whenever someone passes within a light-year of us."

Pax only made a scoffing noise of disgust.

"Approaching ship, identify yourself," Kade said into the comms microphone. Computer generated masking lowered and flattened his voice, turning it odd and mechanical sounding.

There was a pause, during which the door opened again, grinding on its tracks, and Draven came in. "What is it this time?" he asked, his heavy brow furrowed.

"Not sure yet," Hunter said tersely.

On the small vid-screen above the main control console, the chaotic stream of code indicating a secure, scrambled signal coalesced into the pixelated image of a human man with brown eyes, sharp features, and shoulder-length black hair. The tension coiling Hunter's shoulders and back relaxed as the familiar figure spoke.

"Who the hell do you think it is, Kade?" Ash asked rhetorically, the corners of his broad mouth turning down. "Nice voice masking, by the way. Did you buy that distortion unit off the back of a hover-van?"

Kade flipped the switch controlling the voice masking to the off position with a crisp, irritated flick of his fingers. "In case you failed to notice, *leetha*, you're flying the wrong ship. What did you expect?"

Ash looked sour. "Yeah, well. About that. Kind of a long story. And not a terribly interesting one, I'm afraid. Not compared to what I really need to tell you. Let me get this bird down and docked so I can grace you with my presence face to face."

He looked off to the side, reaching for something on his instrument panel. The low-res image revealed an ugly bruise blooming over one high cheekbone for only an instant before the transmission cut off. Beside Hunter, Draven made a sharp hissing noise as he sucked in a breath.

Hunter ignored him, well used to both Ash's knocks and bruises, and Draven's subsequent sniping about them. The ship Ash was piloting was a standard courier—nothing fancy. The vessel's codes had been wiped; it was running unregistered, which told Hunter that Ash must have acquired it on the fly. Otherwise, he would have taken time to forge new registration—child's play to a seasoned tech-worm like their mercurial human ally.

If Ash were being pursued by anyone, he would have said. Well, actually, if he were being pursued he wouldn't have come here in the first place. The fact that he was here at all meant he must have something vitally important and time-sensitive to relay. Something that couldn't be entrusted to subspace communications.

Though there was nothing to suggest any connection between Ash's abrupt arrival and the shuttle crash, the proximity of the two events made the back of Hunter's neck prickle. And Hunter had only managed to stay alive as long as he had because of his uncommonly good instincts.

The sleek little courier ship was already descending, coming to a neat landing cozied up to the compound's main airlock. Ash was quick and thorough as always, shutting down the ship's systems and deploying an umbilical link to the base. Before a quarter-cycle had passed, he was striding into the control room, wearing a glare that sat poorly on his finely drawn features.

"What the hell happened to my e-suit?" he asked. "If you think I'm flopping around in a Vithii-sized suit whenever I have to leave the base, you're all barking mad."

"Your *e-suit*?" Draven asked. "What the *hell* happened to your *face*?"

The human curse word rolled oddly off of Draven's tongue. Hunter stifled a sigh. Draven knew perfectly well what had happened to Ash. They all did. Indeed, Ash turned to him and adopted an exaggerated pose of contemplation, chin resting in his fingers, irony rolling off him in waves. In the cold light of the control room, the bruising on his cheek stood out starkly, along with finger-shaped marks around his throat.

"Hmm, what could possibly have happened?" he said, milking every word. "Maybe the same thing that happens pretty much every time I have to go roll around in the dirt to dig up information."

A rumble sounded low in Draven's chest. "Oh, so there was dirt involved this time?"

"Enough," Hunter said sharply, before the sniping could escalate from opening salvos to something more intense. "Draven, put a spanner in it. Ash, what have you got for us?"

Ash's expression went from annoyed to grim in the space of a heartbeat. He looked around. "Where's Ryder? Do you want her here before I start?"

"She's otherwise engaged," Hunter said. "I'll brief her afterward, or you can."

With a nod, Ash dropped into one of the molded duraplast chairs, and blew out a breath. "Right. So we've all known for a while about the whispers of something big coming—a move from the Regime that will topple things in the Capital into full-blown interspecies conflict."

Hunter nodded. The government had been cracking down ruthlessly on the human residents of Ilarius for months now, ever since the last vote had shifted the balance of power to a Vithii supermajority in all three houses of the legislature. Things had been tense, with widespread rioting and brutal police actions against human civilians in response. It was still—arguably—within the realm of the rule of law. But only *just*.

Lately, though, there had been rumbles of something darker. Something that would change the course of things in a way that could never be undone.

"That's not news. It's been inevitable ever since the last election," Kade observed, bitterness making the words come out cold and hard.

Ash shrugged, still grim. "Maybe. But it was all conjecture and fear mongering until something concrete came out. Well, now it's out. The Premiere has been secretly developing a bio-weapon for the last six months. It's ready now, and he intends to deploy it. Sooner, rather than later, I gather."

"Deploy it where?" Kade asked, his cynical facade giving way to a look of sick queasiness.

"The Capital. Where else? He wants to make a statement."

"That's madness," said Kade. "There are more Vithii in the Capital city than humans. It doesn't make any sense."

"Actually, it makes perfect sense," Ash said tightly, "since the bio-weapon only affects humans."

THREE

Silence fell.

"Shite," Draven said after a long beat.

"Bio-agents are a coward's weapon," Pax said, his flat voice sounding odd in the charged atmosphere.

Ash shrugged, his hands coming up to rub at his shoulders as if he were cold. "Yeah? So what's your point, big man?" The human took a deep breath, as if to shake himself free of the heavy silence. "Anyway, that's what I've got. Unfortunately, while I was busy elsewhere, the security sneaks managed to track me down through the hypernet and link to my hopper's systems. They must have been more adept than the usual government hacks, because the emergency failsafe kicked in and fried the system to prevent them from getting anything out of it. It's totally bricked, so I had to, er, creatively liberate a courier to get off-planet."

Hunter frowned. "Can they get anything physical from the hopper? Do they know where it is?"

Ash shook his head. "Nah. If they find it at all, it'll just be a burned out hulk. The fire from when the computer system roasted itself will have destroyed any DNA evidence, and the ship itself is clean of anything incriminating."

Hunter didn't question him further. If the human said it wasn't a problem, then it wasn't a problem.

"So. Anyway," Ash said. "I should probably split. I've got a business to run—"

Draven straightened to his full height. "You're not going back to the Capital."

Ash shot him a look that implied he had some sort of mental deficit. "Well, *of course* I'm going back to the Capital. I'm not going to find out anything useful skulking around out here, now am I?"

Hunter heard Draven draw breath to say something else and cut him off. "See Ryder in the medbay before you go, Ash. We've had our own bit of excitement recently. I'd be curious for your take on it."

It was very possible that their mysterious prisoner would open up to another human, saving Hunter the necessity for a protracted and potentially messy interrogation. One that he was decidedly *not* looking forward to, with his fucked-up instincts screaming at him to protect his vulnerable female prisoner rather than intimidate her.

Ash raised an eyebrow. "Sure," he said easily, curiosity plain on his face. "Care to share a bit more detail?"

Hunter waved a hand, impatient to start talking with the others about plans and contingencies. "Ryder can explain it. Send her up here when you're done."

Ash gave a shrug and nodded, heading for the door with a final brief glare at Draven, whose burning eyes followed him until the door closed behind him, cutting him off from view.

In the medbay, Skye continued to watch the female Vithii medic with wary eyes. After a few minutes, the blaring alarm went quiet, and she relaxed by increments. Shortly afterward, a comm unit in the corner beeped, and the woman answered it.

"About time you remembered me," she said. "How worried should I be?"

Skye couldn't make out the reply, but the woman softened visibly. "Right. Good. You need me there for anything?"

Another crackling reply, and she grunted and cut off the link.

"Crisis averted," she said in a dry voice, returning to Skye's cot. "Now, aside from elevated blood pressure, racing pulse, and whatever the fuck is going on with your brain chemistry at the moment, how do you feel?"

Skye swallowed. "What happened to me?" she asked in lieu of an answer. She was in such a deep hole right now that she couldn't see a way out, but one thing was clear. She couldn't let these Vithii know about the data crystal she was carrying. Maybe if she could get them talking, she would learn something she could use to escape, or at least get a message out.

Yeah. Right. Sure you will. A message to who, exactly?

Her father was dead. Her stepmother was being held in a Vithii prison. It was very likely that her foster brother had been captured or killed while trying to act as a decoy for her.

She shook off the unhelpful internal monologue and glared at the Vithii woman with as much bravado as she could muster.

It must not have been very effective, because the woman only snorted.

"What *happened* to you?" her Vithii captor echoed. "You crashed a shuttle and broke approximately one-third of the bones in your body. Not to mention the concussion, the partially collapsed lung, the spinal swelling, and the perforated bile duct. Oh, yes… and the bruised kidneys."

Skye took in the recitation with a growing feeling of shock. The numbness was a relief in some ways, dulling her panic and the sharp ache of grief. She knew it would also dull her wits, though, and she couldn't afford that. She made a concerted effort to take the words on board and sort through them.

She still felt terribly weak, but she was not in any appreciable pain. A terrible thought struck, and her eyes flew up to the woman's. "How long—?" If she had been here for weeks—

"About sixty cycles," said her captor.

A little more than two days. It still wasn't too late. But… those injuries the woman had rattled off…

"Why am I not dead?" Skye asked. "Why do I feel… mostly okay?"

"I used nanotech to heal the worst of the damage. You're welcome, by the way."

Nausea flooded Skye's stomach. "You used *bots* on me?" She knew what the Vithii did with nanotech. Had this woman turned her into some kind of laboratory horror while she was unconscious and unable to defend herself? She shuddered, trying to focus inward—to see if anything in her body felt wrong. Felt like… *not her.*

The woman rolled her eyes. "You can stop looking at me like some kind of monster, girl. We programmed them to deactivate and disassemble themselves once they'd finished putting you back together. They're mostly carbon anyway. Your body will flush out the parts that aren't within a day or two."

Skye wondered if the 'we' referred to The Rook, or to someone else—but it seemed unlikely that the woman would tell her if she asked.

"Oh," she said instead. "Well, I… um… guess they worked pretty well. My muscles are weak, but everything seems pretty much how it should be aside from that. Maybe you could… let me get up now?"

Not that she had a snowball's chance in hell of overpowering this two-meter tall, hard-muscled woman and getting away. But she was painfully aware that her chances would be even worse once The Rook came back. It was probably now or never, and far too much was riding on Skye getting free. Getting *out of here*, before it was too late.

"I think not," said her captor. "For one thing, the escape plan you're so transparently considering will look pretty stupid when your knees buckle and you end up in a heap on the floor."

The numb wash of hopelessness rose higher. She *had* to think of something. But there was nothing. That she had escaped from the Regime compound and survived the subsequent shuttle crash was a miracle. Yet all it really meant was that things were going to fall apart a few days later than if she'd simply died in a fireball. Everything depended on her, but she hadn't been fast enough. Strong enough. *Good* enough.

Why did you put this on me, Daddy? she thought, grief stabbing through the numbness and settling around her chest like a steel band. *Why me?*

"Look. I need to go get a better idea of what's going on," the Vithii woman was saying. "The water's right next to you. Drink it. We'll see about starting you on nutrient broth when I get back. In the mean time, you might want to spend a few minutes thinking about your answers to some of the obvious questions, like *who are you* and *what are you doing here.*"

Without waiting for a reply, she strode out of the room, the door whooshing shut behind her. Leaving Skye once again alone, and trapped. Out of time and out of options.

———◆———

Ash strode through the warren of corridors toward the outpost's medbay, his mind already on what he'd need to do once he got back to Ilarius. The situation seemed so hopeless that he wasn't at all sure it could be salvaged. Frankly, the only plan that suggested itself right now was trying to pirate the signal of a major media outlet and urge emergency evacuation of all humans in the Capital.

Whether anyone listening would believe him or truly understand the magnitude of the threat, however, was an open question.

He was distracted enough that he nearly walked face first into Ryder as they both rounded a corner at the same time.

"Whoa!" he said, as they each put out a hand to steady the other. "Sorry, doc—I was just coming to see you. Hunter said you had a *situation*."

Ryder's expression was dour. "You could say that." Her eyes narrowed as she took in the state of his face. "You've been playing dangerous games again, *leetha*. I hope whatever you got was worth it."

Ash stifled his sigh. "You could say that," he parroted back at her. "The Premiere is planning on releasing a human-specific bio-weapon in the Capital."

Ryder went pale. "That *man*. May the human gods damn him to their hell. I may have been a doctor once, but I will enjoy seeing him die in agony."

"You're still a doctor," Ash said automatically.

Her face closed off, but her gaze wandered back to his bruises. "Is that you asking me to fix these up for you? Come back to the medbay and I'll see what I can do."

"*No*, that was not me asking for your services, Ryder," Ash said, feeling suddenly tired. "You know they always like to leave their mark where it can be seen. And I may have need of this one for a while longer." He let the instinctive surge of bitterness drain away, as he had so many times before. "Thanks for the offer, though. Tell me about your *situation*, instead."

Ryder still looked unhappy, but she let the subject go, for which he was thankful.

"An old *Dorish*-class shuttle crashed near the base a couple of days ago," she said. "Real museum piece—practically derelict. One human female on board, badly injured. I patched her back together with some of Pax's nanotech, and she's recovering. Waiting for interrogation, now. She doesn't look like military or undercover espionage. She looks like a terrified civvy."

Ash frowned. *Okay*… that was definitely weird.

"Coincidence?" he asked, not sure what else it could reasonably be.

Ryder lifted her broad shoulders and let them drop. "Good question. In fact, maybe it's one you should ask her. She might be willing to spill everything to a sympathetic human ear. Save Hunter having to play the scary bad guy when it's obvious he's dreading it."

Ash raised an eyebrow at that last part, but let it pass.

"Sure," he said, already intrigued by their mystery pilot. "I'll give it a shot. I'm told that charm is one of my defining characteristics."

Ryder snorted. "One of them, maybe. Go on, then—save us some work. Does Hunter need me in the control room?"

"Yeah, they're discussing strategy in light of the new threat," he said. "He wants you in on it, for sure."

"Right," Ryder said. "Let us know if you get anything out of the pilot."

"Of course," Ash said, already turning to continue on to the medbay. Just now, any distraction was welcome. And even in the middle of a crisis, he always had enjoyed a good mystery.

———◆———

Skye looked up as the door whooshed open only minutes after the Vithii woman left, already more than tired of the way the speeding pulse monitor broadcast her fear to everybody within hearing distance.

Instead of The Rook or another Vithii, though, it was a strikingly handsome human man who walked through. He was olive-skinned and dark-haired, with sharp, chiseled features and an easy grace in the way he carried himself.

He smiled when he saw her, and Skye's attention was drawn to the marks of a vicious beating on his face and neck. Was he a prisoner here, too? She caught her breath at the sudden flash of irrational hope upon seeing a fellow human. He might be in roughly the same predicament she was, but he was at least free to walk around. Maybe he could get to a comm unit, or—

"Hey," he said casually.

He stopped a meter or two inside the door—far enough to let it close behind him, but well out of her space.

"Who are you?" she asked breathlessly. "Are you a prisoner, too?"

"They call me Ash," he said, watching her intently with dark brown eyes. His voice was pleasant and softly accented with the round vowels and crisp consonants of Old Earth Britain. "I heard you crashed near the base. Thought I should come by and check on you. Fellow humans and all that, you know?"

Skye bit her lip, unwilling to let anything slip until she could get a better read on him. "Can you... let me up?" she asked. "There's a forcefield."

He blinked, and nodded almost immediately. "Yeah, of course. Hang on, let me find the... *ah*." He entered a command at the console across from the medical cot, and the pressure over her lower body dissipated like mist. "There you go. You might want to give it a minute for your circulation to get going again," he added. "Would you like me to do a quick scan on you? Make sure the bots put everything together in more or less the right order?"

She nodded in relief. "*Prophets*, yes—please. I don't even want to *think* about the fact that she used nanotech on me."

His smile was quick and did not reach his eyes. "Yeah—it's nasty stuff in the wrong hands, for sure. Still, it's better than being dead, am I right?"

That remains to be seen, she thought, but forced herself to smile back. "I guess so."

Ash turned back to the console, typing in more commands with quick fingers. The full-body scanner suspended above the cot hummed into life, playing a thin beam of red light over her from head to toe, and back up again. A few moments later, the image appeared on his screen, annotated with dozens of notes corresponding to different organs and body systems.

He hummed and mumbled to himself under his breath as he skimmed through them. "Mm-hmm… yeah… okay… looks good…" After clicking through a couple more screens, he spoke to her directly, his voice sympathetic. "I bet you feel like you've been through the wringer, but this all looks really good. You're lucky that…" His voice trailed off and he frowned at something on the readout. "Hang on… what's that?"

"What's what?" she asked, the beeping growing faster again.

His frown deepened. "Your earring. It's not an earring. It's a data crystal." Sharp brown eyes settled on her. "So, why are you wearing a lab-grade data crystal as jewelry?"

Her breath caught, the racing heart monitor making her head pound. She was trapped—she had to make a decision *right now* even though she could barely string two thoughts together. Stalling, she swung her legs over the edge of the cot and carefully put weight on them. Her knees wobbled, but held—possibly on the strength of all the adrenaline currently sloshing around in her system.

She took a cautious step, one hand on the rickety little tray table for balance. To her immense relief, the shrill beeping cut off as she moved out of the heart monitor's sensor field.

If she didn't tell him, she wouldn't be any closer to getting the contents of the crystal to safety, where the files could be used before it was too late. And he could overpower her and take it by force if he wanted to, she was sure. If she told him, maybe he could help her. Maybe he would understand how important it was.

"My father… is Dr. Zarian Chantrell," she said. *Was*, reminded the voice in her head. *My father* was *Zarian Chantrell*. She swallowed the lump in her throat that threatened to choke her. "He… worked for the Regime. They forced him to create a weaponized bio-agent that the Premiere plans to use against the human population on Ilarius. He gave me the formula for the antidote and helped me get away before he—" The lump grew, her voice cracking. "Before he was—"

Ash's eyes grew wide, and he cut her off. "Holy shit. Holy *shit*. You have a data crystal with—" He paused, his mouth open like a fish, and dove for the comm unit the Vithii medic had used earlier.

"Hunter!" he barked into the pickup. "Fucking prophets, you need to get down here *right now*!"

"*No!*" Skye cried in dismay. She lunged for him as if to drag him away from the comm, even though the damage had already been done. As the medic had warned, her legs buckled beneath her, and she crashed to the cold metal floor.

FOUR

Ash turned, focusing on her like a dog scenting prey. "Let me look at that crystal. I need to see if we have anything here that will read it. That's old tech."

Skye scrambled backward, betrayal and panic warring for dominance in her gut. "Stay the hell away from me, you *race traitor*!" she hissed. "Do you have any idea what you've just *done*? You've sentenced the humans on Ilarius to death! How *could* you?"

The spineless bastard set his jaw. "On the contrary, you'll be sentencing them to death if you don't hand over that crystal so we can get a look at what's on it."

His words didn't make any sense. The two of them were trapped in a base with Vithii criminals who were about as likely to help them as they were to suddenly sprout wings. They were trapped with *barbarians* that had obviously beaten the hell out of him recently, and the first thing he did was to call their leader? She was reminded of the old human psych lessons from her school days. Stockhelm syndrome, or Stockhold syndrome, or something like that. Prisoners becoming attached to their captors.

He must have gone mad with whatever they'd been doing to him. Her eyes slid over the strangulation marks on his neck. She shuddered and looked away. He was on the other side of the room from her—she had a clear line of sight to the door. She pushed up from the floor and staggered toward it on rubbery legs.

It slid open, only to reveal a solid wall of muscular Vithii male. She half-fell against him, unable to halt her momentum, and large hands grasped her upper arms, keeping her upright as if she weighed nothing. Skye was a tall woman, but The Rook towered over her. The power in his body made heart flutter in fear against her chest like a trapped bird.

She screamed her rage full in his face and tried to knee him in the groin, but the angle was wrong to do any damage. Arresting light green eyes looked down at her from the harsh, brutal lines of his alien face, unimpressed. His grip never faltered.

"What the fuck, Ash?" he asked, his gaze flicking over her shoulder to the human traitor behind her.

"Hunter, *she's carrying the antidote to the Regime's bio-agent*. That earring is a data crystal," Ash said, and those disconcerting pale eyes landed on her again.

Skye sagged as the last hope she had of averting destruction slipped away like sand through her fingers. *Oh, gods,* she begged silently. *Just kill me. Just let it be quick.*

He didn't kill her, though.

"Is this true?" he asked.

She squeezed her eyes shut, not wanting to meet that deep, disconcerting gaze. "Fuck you," she whispered. Would he rip her earlobe open to get the crystal? Slice her ear off completely? Nausea flooded her gut.

"Tell us your first name, Ms. Chantrell," Ash said from behind her. "It is Ms. *Chantrell*, correct?"

"What does it matter?" she asked hopelessly. "Just do whatever you're going to do to me. Get it over with."

A new hand settled on her shoulder, and she flinched violently.

"Let's start with getting you back to the medical cot," Ash said, his voice grim, but not threatening. "And then we'll take it from there."

The Rook seemed to hesitate before loosening his grip on her arms, but when he did, Ash slung one of them over his shoulder and helped her back to the thrice-damned cot, where the *fucking* heart monitor immediately started beeping again.

"Cut that off," said The Rook. Was his real name Hunter? Ash had called him Hunter.

The noise went silent. *Small mercies.* At least now, they wouldn't hear how panicked she was as they readied the torture instruments, or whatever they were going to do to her.

"You want me to sedate her again so you can get the crystal?" It was the medic. Skye hadn't even realized that she was here as well.

"No," said The Rook. "We need her awake. She may have additional information."

"Are you going to torture me?" she asked, the heavy numbness from earlier returning. She welcomed it, knowing that dissociation was all that would keep her sane through what was to come. *If it held*.

A furrow formed in The Rook's heavy brow. "Oh, for—" he began, only to cut himself off with a sharp shake of the head. He addressed the others. "Leave us for a few moments."

A bone-deep chill settled over Skye as the others moved to the room's single entrance and walked through, Ash giving her earring a final, longing glance as he left. The door slid shut behind them, leaving her alone with the most dangerous man in the Seven Systems. There was only one reason she could think of that he wouldn't want witnesses.

"You're going to rape me," she said, the words coming out heavy and flat. Devoid of life.

A look of cold scorn crossed his coarse features, and his tone was one of utter contempt. "I prefer my sex partners to be begging before I take them, little sparrow."

She lifted her chin. "I will never beg, you vicious Vithii bastard." She wondered if that was a promise she would be able to keep, once the pain started.

He raised an eyebrow. "Does the sparrow have talons? You'd do better to use them against the Regime than against us, if so."

"What do you know about it, hiding out here in a deserted outpost?" she demanded, hopelessness hanging over her like a pall.

The Rook scoffed. "What does the Shadow Wing know about fighting the Regime? Such a question. The Shadow Wing exists for nothing else."

Now it was her turn to scoff. "Don't make me laugh. You're criminals. The worst Ilarius has to offer. The only thing you care about is stealing and killing."

He paced slowly around the perimeter of the medbay, his movements graceful as a tiger's. Skye watched him warily, feeling every inch the frightened, fluttering sparrow he'd accused her of being, despite her brave words.

"Consider a group," he began, "dedicated to hurting the Regime—weakening it in any way possible. Through theft, sabotage, or outright violence, if need be. What might those in power do to retaliate? To minimize that group's power and influence?"

"I have no idea what you're getting at. You've committed horrific crimes. Done terrible things to innocent people."

"Have I?" asked The Rook. "And wherever would you have heard such information, sparrow?"

"From the news, of course," she said, his apparent desire to talk rather than torture knocking her off-balance. "Your picture was plastered all over the holovids barely more than a week ago." She laughed bitterly, without a trace of amusement. "I recall thinking at the time that my father would have been better off sending the data files to you than dumping them on me. That was right before I remembered that you were a Vithii swine who would probably toss the antidote into a wormhole and throw a party to celebrate while the humans in the Capital vomited up their own stomach lining and bled out through their eyeballs."

He ignored the last part. "Ah, yes. The *news*. And who controls the news services, these days?"

She blinked. "Well… the Regime does."

"Of course it does." The scorn was back in his voice. "And it suits the Regime very well to paint its opponents as dangerous criminals who must be captured or killed at any cost to protect the public."

Skye opened her mouth, trying to find a chink in his argument. Ash's face floated across her memory, with its livid bruises and strangulation marks. "Yeah… well… I might find it a lot easier to believe that you're some kind of Robin Hood hiding out here in the middle of nowhere with your band of Merry Men if you weren't beating the shit out of the only other human on the base."

Shock touched his expression, followed by a flash of real anger, quickly hidden behind that cold mask. "No one here has injured Ash," he said.

"Yeah, of course they haven't," she said. "I'm sure he just fell down the stairs or something. Or maybe you have old-fashioned doorknobs here? Not that he really strikes me as the clumsy type."

The Rook stared at her in apparent consternation. A moment later, he flipped the switch on the comm unit. "Ash, come back in, please."

She gave him a look of incredulity at the *please*. Ash must have been waiting right outside the door, because he returned within seconds.

"Yeah, boss?" he asked. "You got the crystal yet? It occurred to me we could probably cobble together a functioning reader using parts from the downed shuttle. *Dorish*-class technology is from about the same era as that data crystal tech."

"Who injured you, *leetha*?" The Rook asked evenly.

Skye glanced back and forth between the two men, taken aback by the apparent affection behind the nickname. A *leetha* was an animal from the Vitharan home planet, not unlike an Old Earth antelope. It actually wasn't a bad analogy for Ash's sleek, rangy grace.

Ash looked at the Vithii male in surprise, his eyes narrowing. "You want to do this *now*, Hunter? Seriously?"

"I'm not asking for myself," The Rook continued. "Our... guest... has been making assumptions."

Ash's gaze moved to her, understanding dawning—followed closely by horror. "Oh. Gods, no. You thought—?" He seemed to shake himself free of his surprise. "Well, I guess you would, under the circumstances." He brushed his knuckles gently over the ugly dark marks and swelling on his face, wincing a bit as he did so. "But, no. This little memento is courtesy of the Vithii adjunct to the Premiere's Clandestine Operations office."

Skye stared at him, trying to twist her understanding of whatever the hell was happening here until it fit the facts. "You... got in a fistfight with a member of the Regime?"

The Rook made a small, choked noise.

"Not... exactly," Ash hedged, sounding suddenly tired. "Let's just stick with the important part, which is that no one here would lay a hand on me in anger. Well—except maybe Kade, but I still maintain that the whole thing with the open lift shaft and the escape through the sewers was *not my fault*."

Skye was still feeling muddled, and knew that she was at least two steps behind in the conversation. "So... you're claiming that you are not, in fact, criminals, and that instead, you're actually working against the Regime?"

"Oh, we're criminals, sure enough," Ash said. "The courier ship I've got docked outside the airlock is unashamedly stolen, for one thing."

"But we are *most definitely* working against the Regime," said The Rook, and the sneer in his voice at the final word was perhaps the most convincing to Skye.

"So," Ash continued, "you see—we're all on the same side here. Which is why I really, really need to get a look at that data crystal. Time is not our friend at the moment."

She looked between them. One hulking and powerful, one elegant and handsome—both of them obviously comfortable with each other. Perhaps even fond of each other. Did she dare trust everything to them? What was the alternative?

"You already knew about the bio-weapon," she accused. "How?"

Ash raised an eyebrow. "Information is my stock in trade," he said. A hint of bitterness laced the words. "That particular gem came courtesy of the aforementioned adjunct to the Clandestine Operations office in an… unguarded moment."

"A question for a question, little sparrow," The Rook interjected before she could respond. "Why is an unarmed civilian with an ancient, derelict shuttle carrying the most valuable data files in the system?"

It was the moment of truth. Should she speak? Did she have a choice? Suddenly, the reality of her situation slammed into her with all the subtlety of a full-strength tractor beam, and she began to shake.

"I wish to hell I knew," she whispered. "Gods and prophets above… I'm an *accountant*. A fucking *accountant*. I don't have the first idea what to do now, and because of me, everyone in the Capital is going to die."

Hunter watched as the human woman seemed to crumple in on herself, trembling violently. His hands twitched, instinct trying to propel him toward her. He quashed the impulse without mercy.

You'll just frighten her worse.

Ash had no such compunctions, and came forward to place a supportive hand on her shoulder, crouching down to meet the frightened blue eyes that suddenly seemed huge in her pale face.

"Hey," he said. "Hey, easy now. We're all here for the same reason—to take down the Regime. We just need to trust each other, all right?"

Hunter was appalled to find himself fighting the urge to step forward and drag Ash away from the distraught female—to thrust himself between them and snarl at his human ally until he relinquished any claim to her and slunk away. His stomach dropped, the shock of the sudden compulsion enough to drag him back to rationality.

Oh, *fuck* no. He was *not* dealing with a mating drive in the middle of apocalyptic biological warfare and genocide. Genetic imperative or no, that would be *batshit fucking insane*. Kade would string him upside down from his big toes with high tensile wire, and shout at him until his eardrums bled. And he'd be totally justified in doing so.

She was a terrified civvy, so far out of her depth she couldn't even see the shore. Not to mention being the *wrong fucking species*.

Now, she was looking back and forth between him and Ash, obviously teetering on the edge of trusting them. He needed to keep his mouth shut, not do anything to terrify her further, and let Ash work his magic. Even if Hunter had to swallow the growl rumbling at the back of his throat while he was doing it.

"I…" she started hesitantly. "Like I said… I'm Zarian Chantrell's daughter. The Regime forced him to design the bio-agent. They had his wife—my stepmother—in custody and threatened her if he didn't cooperate. I guess they also had my foster brother and me under surveillance, in case they had to use us as leverage, too."

"But your father also designed an antidote to the bio-weapon?" Ash prompted.

She nodded slowly. "He kept it a secret from them. But eventually, he managed to get a message out to Temple—my foster brother. Anyway, Temple and I were allowed family visitation with Dad for my birthday. He gave Temple a decoy file, and slipped me the real one disguised as a birthday gift of jewelry. He'd arranged for me to steal a decommissioned shuttle that was being stored in the hangar at the complex, but he—"

She cut herself off, and swallowed hard.

"Anyway, they were monitoring us, of course. Most of the guards followed Temple, but two came after me. A blast from one of their fighters caught my engines just as I entered the wormhole gate at the edge of the system. I was flung randomly out of the vortex, and ended up in your gravity well. You… know the rest, I guess."

Ash looked over at him, and Hunter nodded, once more in control of himself. *Thankfully*.

"That explains how you ended up here," Hunter said. "It wasn't coincidence after all."

The woman frowned, her gaze flicking from one to the other of them. "What do you mean?"

Ash answered. "You entered a gate with malfunctioning engines. Hunter chose this place because it's situated near a weak spot in the wormhole system. There's no gate nearby, but with the right timing and a bit of cheating with your engine settings, you can get a ship through the subspace barrier and back into realspace without anyone being able to detect the passage. Your failing engines replicated that process, and spat you out here on our doorstep."

"Oh," she said on a faint breath. "I guess that does explain why the guards chasing me couldn't simply follow me and finish the job."

"It does," Hunter said, pleased that her appearance here was not tied to their presence by anything more sinister than damaged engines and an eccentricity of subspace travel. "Though if they look long and hard enough, they might detect the weak spot in the system and follow it here. We may need to evacuate as a precaution."

Ash's expression turned grim. "We need that crystal, Ms. Chantrell. We have to move, or this whole thing is going to go belly up on us."

The woman was still shaking, but she clenched one hand into a hard fist, trying to steady it. "My name is Skye," she said after a short pause. "And may the gods forgive me if I'm making a mistake."

With that, she reached up and removed the crystal earring, fumbling at it for a moment with trembling fingers. Hunter hid a sigh of relief at her capitulation, and Ash practically pounced on the tiny, faceted stone when she proffered it.

He was out the door an instant later, no doubt heading at top speed for the nearest lab. The woman—*Skye*—wrapped her arms around herself as if to combat a sudden chill. Hunter was caught between the intense desire to be elsewhere, and an equally strong desire never to leave her presence again.

She looked at him with flat, exhausted eyes. "Are you really going to help? This isn't some kind of a trick?"

"We're really going to help," he managed.

"Why?" she asked.

Broken bodies, twisted and burned, tangled together on the pavement. Shockingly red human blood soaking into the fabric of his trousers from an expanding puddle as he crashed to his knees next to them, heart pounding in his throat.

Pain filled blue-gray eyes trying to focus on his green ones. Lips moving, struggling to form words as frothy blood bubbled up. "Hun… ter. Love… you, sweetheart. Now run…"

He shoved the memory down, burying it where it belonged in the tight, dark space behind his ribcage.

"Because the Regime has killed enough innocent humans already," was all he said.

Something opened up behind the woman's eyes—some deep abyss that seemed poised to consume her whole. She swallowed, visibly pulling herself back from the brink.

"Yeah," she agreed, the word a hoarse whisper. "It has."

FIVE

Skye watched the powerful, dangerous looking Vithii whom she'd been conditioned by the media to fear as he left the medbay, pausing for an instant in the open doorway as if he might say something, or perhaps look back at her over his shoulder. He did neither.

A moment later, he was replaced by the female medic and two more towering Vithii males that she had not seen before. Skye clenched the edge of the cot with white knuckles to keep from flinching at their approach, knowing she needed to get over this terrified prey animal shit *right now*. It might turn out to be the stupidest thing she'd ever done, but for better or worse, she'd thrown her lot in with theirs.

It was still totally possible that she'd made the worst mistake of her life, but as her brain slowly started to kick itself back into gear after her injuries and the shock of everything that had happened to her, she began to piece things together a bit more rationally.

If they'd wanted her dead, they wouldn't have gone to the trouble of patching her together after the shuttle crash. If they wanted to hurt her, the logical time to do it would have been when they so obviously wanted the data crystal and she was refusing to give it to them. The medic had even offered to sedate her rather than letting one of them simply grab her and rip the thing out of her ear.

The taller of the two newcomers looked down at her with cold gray eyes. He was slender by Vithii standards, which admittedly wasn't saying much. Tight, corded muscle still bulged from his chest and biceps. His face was more sharply chiseled than The Rook's. He had an air of having been stripped down to essentials… worn away until nothing was left but hard, unyielding stone.

"So," he said, "you're a mad scientist's daughter who daylights as an accountant and plays at being a spy on your nights off. *Badly*, I might add." He shook his head in evident disgust. "Not even Ash could make this kind of shit up."

"Yeah, he could," said the other one, a small mountain of a male who looked like he could bend durasteel rods in his bare, meaty hands. Where The Rook's eyes were a striking pale green, and those of the man who'd just spoken were gray, his were a strange light hazel, shot through with gold.

"Did you two actually need something, or did you just come here to gawp and scare the shit out of my patient?" groused the medic as she ran a handheld sensor over Skye's head and torso.

Skye set her jaw, more than done with being the victim. "I think I'm past the point of being scared shitless, thanks," she said. "That mental circuit blew a while ago. Your… leader? The Rook? He said you were going to help me fight the Regime. Is that true?"

The barest hint of amusement pulled at the tall one's expression before he covered it. "As soon as you said *fight the Regime,* I imagine you had Hunter on board. And if he's on board, then the rest of us will inevitably be dragged along for the ride." He studied her for a moment. "You're really Zarian Chantrell's daughter, then? I read his paper a few years ago on the molecular chemistry of Vithii neurotonin receptors. It was impressive work. At least, I think it was. I was admittedly fairly drunk at the time."

His companion snorted. "Everyone knows you do your best work drunk, Kade." His attention turned back to Skye. "We need to figure out logistics. Ash is trying to cobble together a reader for the data crystal."

"Which reminds me," interjected the one called Kade. His attention turned to the medic. "He's plenty pissed at you right now, Ryder. He had to borrow your e-suit to go out to the shuttle wreck. Apparently *someone* took a protoplaser to the only human-sized suit we had."

"I told Hunter you'd buy him a new one," said the Vithii woman, unconcerned.

"*Great.* I'll put it on his birthday wish list." Sarcasm oozed from the words. The barb was obviously innocent repartee, but right now it seemed that every little remark was designed to remind Skye of things she really couldn't afford to think about.

A birthday. Her father. Temple.

She shook herself free of the pit of grief waiting to swallow her. *Not now. Not yet.*

"Banter later," said the golden-eyed Vithii male. "Planning now. I'm Draven, by the way. I've never actually heard of your mad scientist sire, but as long as he could write out a coherent chemical formula we'll do our best to make it and get it where it needs to be."

Hope surged. "You're a chemist?" she asked.

"I'm a gutter rat who grew up cooking drugs for the local cartel," he said. "And as you've probably gathered, Ryder is a medical doctor."

"*Former* medical doctor," growled the Vithii woman.

"Between the two of us, I expect we can tell the difference between a covalent bond and a carbon molecule," Draven continued, as if he hadn't heard her. "We just need someplace to work, and access to the raw materials we'll need. Which, unfortunately, means going back to Ilarius unless someone can come up with an alternative."

"Oh, good," said Kade. "Ilarius again. I can hardly wait."

The medic—*Ryder*—stepped into Skye's line of sight and glared at Kade. "Aren't you due for an injection?"

"Yes, I bloody well am," Kade said. "Fine, I know when I'm not wanted. I'll go see if I can get a long-range comm message through to some of my old contacts." He sighed. "This is going to end up costing me a metric fuck-ton of money, isn't it?"

"Yes," said Draven.

"It's not as though you can't afford it," added Ryder.

Kade's gray eyes landed on Skye, and she covered a flinch. Potential ally or no, the man was still intimidating as hell—almost as much so as The Rook himself. She made herself meet his gaze.

"Thank you," she said, pleased that her voice didn't waver. "It seems I owe you a debt of gratitude."

He held her eyes for a long moment, as if testing whether she would look away. "Yes," he said, the words without inflection. "You do."

With that, he left, presumably to go talk to his contacts, or perhaps get whatever injection he apparently needed. The others didn't comment, and Skye got the impression that they were used to his prickly behavior.

A nutrient pack appeared in front of her—one of those old self-warming pouches that always tasted like over-salted tomato soup, no matter what flavor it was actually supposed to be.

"Drink," said Ryder. "If you keep it down we'll try solid food in a bit. Draven, ask whatever you were planning to ask and get out. She needs more rest."

Draven shrugged. "Just wondered if your sire gave you any useful information beyond what's on the crystal. The delivery system is going to be the real challenge in this."

Ryder snorted, clearly conveying her opinion of that assessment. Honestly, Skye couldn't disagree. There were a hell of a lot of challenges to overcome before they reached the point of distributing the antidote to the humans in the Capital.

"He didn't," she said. "We were under surveillance the whole time. He couldn't talk freely. I've been thinking about it a lot, though. And it occurred to me that the entire Capital city relies on a single water system."

Draven made a considering noise.

"There's no safe surface water to speak of. Not on the northern continent," she continued. "So everyone pretty much has to drink from the public system—human and Vithii alike. Would there be a way to introduce the antidote into the water supply somehow?"

Ryder finally put aside the medical sensor she'd been using to scan Skye and leaned a hip against the console across from the narrow cot. "Effective dosage level is the key," she said. "That's a huge amount of water you're talking about."

"Hmm," Draven said. "Yeah. Not sure it would be practical to produce and transport that kind of volume, especially since the authorities are almost guaranteed to be on high alert."

Skye's heart sank.

Ryder tapped her fingers on the edge of the console where she was leaning. "What if we could utilize materials already present in the system?"

Draven frowned. "All that's in the system is water."

"Yeah," Ryder agreed. "Water. Hydrogen and oxygen. And carbon filtration media. Add a source of nitrogen and a few trace minerals…"

Skye looked at her in confusion, but Draven's face lit up in understanding before she could ask any questions.

"You're talking about using nanotech to synthesize the antidote on the fly, from right inside the system," he murmured. "That's actually brilliant, Ryder. Also a bit crazy, but… crazy in a brilliant way."

"I blame the company I've been keeping lately," Ryder said in a dry tone. "So, I guess we need to talk to Pax. We'll have to get the nanobots breeding more nanobots first, before we worry about getting them to synthesize our compound for us." She pointed a finger in Skye's face. "You. Get some rest. We'll probably have to move fast once we do move, and you're not strong enough yet."

Skye blinked. "You expect me to *sleep* at a time like this?" she asked incredulously.

The medic looked at her, unimpressed. "Since I put a sedative in your nutrient broth, I'd call it a safe bet, yes."

"You *what*?" Anger and worry struggled for dominance, but indeed, Skye could already feel warm, comfortable darkness lapping at the edges of her turbulent thoughts. "I can't be unconscious while the rest of you are planning straget... startegy—" Her tongue, thick and unresponsive, stumbled over the word. "*Stra... te... gy.*"

Ryder huffed out a breath. "Really? I think you'll find that you can."

"Damn you," Skye said very carefully and distinctly, right before she slumped into the other woman's strong hands. Ryder lowered her carefully to the cot, and Skye was out cold before her head touched the pillow.

⸺◆⸺

When she woke up, the first thing she noticed was that she felt considerably stronger than she had before. The second thing was that there seemed to be quite a bit of activity going on. The third thing was that she was really, really hungry. And the fourth was that she needed rather desperately to use the lav.

All of these appeared to be generally positive developments, so she cleared her throat and said, "Erm... hello?"

The two figures huddled over a readout screen across the room looked up and glanced over their shoulders at her.

One of them was Ryder, but Skye's breath caught when the glare of the harsh overhead lights illuminated a filigree of shining metal implants nearly covering half of the other Vithii's face.

A cyborg. She was in the same room as a cyborg.

Well, genius, where did you think they got nanotech from?

She swallowed, knowing that the rational part of her mind was undeniably talking sense. But she also knew what Vithii cyborg soldiers were capable of doing.

They were berserkers. Mindless weapons to be pointed at the enemy and let loose, while the non-augmented meatbags stood safely out of the way and watched destruction rain down. The being currently watching her from across the room with flat, disinterested eyes could snap her spine like a twig. It wouldn't even make him break a sweat.

Not that he probably needed to sweat, with all the tech swimming around in his system.

He eyed her as a human might eye a mildly irritating bug. "What are you staring at?" he asked. A flat, metallic rasp lent his voice a faintly mechanical tone.

Skye opened and closed her mouth a couple of times before she could make words come out. "S-sorry. I… uh. I guess you must be Pax? I'm Skye. Th-thanks for helping save me. When my shuttle crashed, I mean."

Silence stretched, and she swallowed hard.

Ryder's sigh broke it. "Don't terrify the civvy, Pax. It's not cute, and it's not funny."

The cyborg warrior raised an eyebrow, metal glinting as his expression shifted. "It is a little bit funny." The words were delivered in that same mechanical monotone.

Skye relaxed a bit, still wary, but reassured by Ryder's casual rebuke and Pax's response.

"I really am sorry," she reiterated. "It was rude of me to stare."

Ryder had pity on her. "The propaganda machine casts a wide net. And to be fair, a lot of what you've heard about Vithii cyborgs is true. Pax is a bit of a special case. Now. How do you feel? Hunter wants to move soon."

Skye took stock. Still hungry. Still needed to pee. "Better. Starving. But first, is there a lav I can use?"

"Turn right in the hallway and go two doors down," Ryder said. "Oh, and avoid the sink on the right side. Something's growing in it and I haven't been able to determine what it is, or why bleach compound won't kill it. You okay to walk?"

When she tentatively slid from the now-familiar medical cot, her legs felt much steadier than they had earlier. "Yeah. Thanks. I'll be back shortly, unless the right-hand sink gets me."

Ryder saluted her with a quirked eyebrow and a small upward tic of the lips. Skye made her way carefully to the lav, reveling in the feeling of her limbs obeying her brain's commands more or less the way they were supposed to.

She used the too-tall, awkwardly shaped latrine, washed her hands in the left hand sink after giving the one on the right a cautious side-eye, and splashed water on her face. After returning to the medbay and eating the reconstituted rations Ryder shoved at her, she felt almost like a functioning human being again.

Apparently, her timing on that front was pretty good, because a council of war appeared to be convening elsewhere in the station. After a brief conversation over the comm unit, Pax left without a word.

Ryder glanced up at her and made a shooing motion. "Go on. Follow him. I've got to stay and babysit these bots so they don't go all 'gray goo' on us. But I expect you'll want to be in on this meeting. Ash managed to cobble together a data reader and he's downloading your files now."

A jolt of excitement banished the last of Skye's residual weakness, and she hurried after Pax's massive form. The cyborg disappeared through a door at what must have been the outer edge of the station. Skye ducked in after him, only to be confronted by a room full of intently focused, powerful men, every one of whom looked up to stare at her as the door screeched shut behind her on rusty tracks.

She froze for an instant as her eyes flicked from one to the other of them and finally caught on The Rook's pale green gaze. It was oddly difficult to tear herself away.

No more fear, she thought. *You should be dead a dozen times over already. What's left to be afraid of?*

"Ryder said you were about to read the files," she said.

She was rewarded by a tight smile from Ash. "The moment of truth, yes. We'll see if there's any data corruption… always assuming this bodge-up of mine doesn't blow a fuse first."

He was hovering over a hastily constructed jumble of tech that looked like the aftermath of a small explosion in a spaceport junk shop. It was sitting on a lab bench, wired into one of the station's terminals. Skye screwed up her courage and walked forward until she could see the screen properly over Ash's shoulder. The small hairs on the back of her neck prickled as The Rook shifted behind her.

The terminal was currently spouting gibberish. After a few tweaks from Ash's deft fingers, though, it resolved into a standard representation of file architecture. The silence was absolute except for the quiet hum of a hard drive as the files downloaded. Ash clicked through screens until the display filled with scrolling lines of chemical formula.

"So, Draven?" he asked. "This make sense to you?"

SIX

Draven shouldered his way forward and scanned the slow march of green symbols against the black background. Skye held her breath. If she had come all this way, only to find that the files were useless…

"Yeah," Draven said slowly, and dragged a finger over some lines of output. "Yeah, I can see what he was doing here. It's more of an antitoxin than a vaccine. Blocks the cell receptors so the toxin from the bio-agent can't bind to them. See? Here… and here. Ryder'll have a better idea of the particulars."

The air escaped Skye's lungs in a relieved *whoosh*. "Thank the gods," she breathed.

The Rook's deep, rough voice behind her shoulder made her jump. "Can you synthesize this compound?"

Draven shrugged, still scanning the ever-changing lines of data. "Between the two of us, I don't see why not—given the right facilities and raw materials. I doubt we could manage it here. Not enough space, and not enough equipment. I need a chemistry lab, not an astrophysics lab built in my great-grandsire's time."

Skye's attention moved to Kade, who pushed away from the bench he was leaning against and regarded Draven, arms crossed. "Well, then," said the hard-eyed Vithii male, "let's get this place packed up and get our asses back to Ilarius. I've got a meeting scheduled with someone who might be able to help, assuming we don't get vaped by the security forces on the way in."

"This meeting isn't with Jago, is it?" asked The Rook.

"Of course it's with fucking Jago," Kade answered. "Who else is gonna provide a fully decked out lab with hardly any notice to a bunch of known criminals?"

"You know how much I hate that bastard." The Rook glared across at Kade.

Kade glared back. "I know how much he hates *you*, if that's what you mean."

"Who's Jago?" Skye asked, and the pair broke away from their stare-down to look at her, as if surprised she'd spoken.

"A businessman," said Kade.

"A back-stabbing son of a whore with an ego the size of a red giant," said The Rook.

"Who is also a businessman," Kade added.

"What kind of business?" Skye asked, mildly fascinated by the exchange.

Draven snorted. "Drugs, of course. Hence the lab. Also, prostitutes." His gold-flecked eyes slid to Ash and flickered away again so quickly Skye wasn't sure she'd really seen it.

"Occasionally weapons, as well," said Kade, unperturbed.

The brief, insane urge to make some comment about *birds of a feather* rose, but she stamped it down. There was *brave*, and then there was *stupid*. The Rook's obvious distaste for this Jago person piqued her curiosity, though.

Instead, she focused on the practical. "So, you think he'll let us use a drug lab to synthesize the antidote?"

Kade shrugged a shoulder. "For the right money, why not? If it's more profitable for him than the drugs he could churn out over the same period of time, he'd be a fool not to."

"And you've got the money to make it more profitable for him?" she asked.

Kade's expression could hardly have been called *open* before, but at her words, it closed off as if a blast door had slammed shut—cold and hard.

It was The Rook who answered. "As Ash said, we *are* criminals. But Kade is the one with a head for business. He takes care of the finances. If he says there's enough, then there's enough."

He was still standing close enough to her that his voice and powerful presence raised gooseflesh on her arms.

She nodded. "All right, so that part's sorted, then. How do we get through the blockade around Ilarius?"

"It's not a strict no-fly zone, by any stretch," said Ash. "You just need to have the right codes and registration on your ship. Or, more to the point, you need to have someone *else's* codes and registration, in our case. Don't worry, I can handle that part."

She digested this for a moment. "So, you're abandoning this outpost completely? You're not coming back?"

Pax looked at her. "Strategic decision. Someone might still come looking for your shuttle. If they find it, best for us to be elsewhere."

It was an existence she could barely imagine—always hiding, always on the run. An existence, she realized with a jolt, that was now hers, as well. "I'm sorry you all have to pull up stakes because of me."

The Rook glanced around at the dusty, rust-stained lab. "Sorry about this place? Not exactly five-star accommodations," he said.

"Besides," added Draven. "That green stuff growing in the lav is starting to make me nervous. Ryder swore that the high-intensity UV blast would get rid of it, but I think it's actually growing faster than before."

A choked noise forced its way up Skye's throat, not really amusement—more of a bubble of hysteria brought on by the complete surreality of the last couple of days. She covered her mouth for a moment, until she was sure she had control again.

"Thank you," she managed. "I… still can't quite believe that you're doing all this."

"Yeah… believe me, you're not alone in that," said Kade, and Skye still couldn't read his expression.

The Rook's eyes pinned hers, deep and clear as the ocean. "Don't thank us yet," he said. "Ash will brief you on what we'll need to do next."

Draven frowned. "If we're going into the under-city, what exactly *are* we going to do with this one, anyway?" He jerked his chin toward her. "Ash, can you keep her with you?"

Ash's mouth twisted into a frown. "Where I'm headed isn't any safer for her than the undercity would be. In fact, it's probably worse."

Draven's scowl was brief, but fierce, and his eyes seemed to rake over the bruises on the human's face. "Well, then—what?"

"Pass her off as your *seelaht*, Hunter," Kade said off-handedly. "No one would question it."

"*No*," said The Rook, and the tone of his rough-velvet voice sent chills along Skye's spine.

Kade rolled his eyes. "Fine. We'll pass her off as *my seelaht*, then. Does it matter?"

In an instant, The Rook was in Kade's face, the two powerful males facing off, practically nose to nose. Kade looked unimpressed, but anger rolled off The Rook in waves, though he didn't move a muscle.

"No," said The Rook. "We will not pass her off as *your seelaht*, Kade."

This time, the shiver that went up Skye's spine brought an unexplained flush of heat with it, rather than a chill.

Kade narrowed his eyes, neither matching The Rook's anger nor backing down. "*Tei'laal*, I don't give two fucks *who* takes her. But someone's going to have to provide a believable reason why we're dragging a human woman to an underworld meeting, and that's a believable reason. So drop the posturing, and make a decision."

A low growl rumbled through The Rook's broad chest, and he took a measured step back, still not breaking eye contact. "I'll think about it," he said, as if the words had been pulled from him.

"You do that," said Kade. "In the mean time, I've got a ship to load."

With that, Kade turned on his heel and left the lab. The Rook threw a burning glance in Skye's direction before dragging his glowing green eyes away.

"Finish what you need to in here, then get yourselves packed and ready to fly. We're leaving at eighteen hundred," he said, before stalking through the door after Kade.

The others had been utterly silent through the brief confrontation. Draven and Pax shared a look, and Draven shrugged. "Right. Packing. Get me a copy of that file as soon as it's ready, Ash."

He left as well, the cyborg close on his heels, leaving Skye alone with Ash in the now-quiet lab.

"What's a *seelaht*?" Skye asked, bewildered.

———◆———

Hunter prowled through the corridors toward the tiny, austere room he'd claimed as his quarters. Everything about the exchange with Kade in the lab had been… *unacceptable*. He should not have re-acted the way he did to Kade's suggestion, which was both an obvious and a practical one.

Yet the idea of him playing at such a thing was sickening, because the human woman obviously still feared him. And yet, it was also seductively—*dangerously*—appealing, while the idea of seeing her collared by Kade, pretending to fawn over him, threatened to unleash a torrent of bloodlust inside Hunter that had no connection to modern-day, civi-lized Vithii society.

Unacceptable.

Kade had no interest in her whatsoever. Less than none. He was also the closest thing to a friend Hunter had. They were both twisted shadows, haunted by demons that would make an innocent like Skye Chantrell cringe away in disgust—and rightly so.

His sick fascination with her needed to end, *right the fuck now*. As the nominal leader of their cohort of misfits and criminals, the others' safety rested on his shoulders. As, apparently, did the lives of tens of thousands of humans living on Ilarius, who were about to be sentenced to a grisly death.

The door to his quarters opened at his approach and slid shut behind him. He ran a hand roughly over his face and dragged fingers through his spiky hair, feeling it spring back into place as they passed. A bark of bitter laughter, like the sound of rusty gears grinding together, rose from his chest. If the unsuspecting humans in the Capital knew whose hands now held their fate, they would flee in terror.

He looked around the bleak, cramped space that had functioned as his temporary home, intent on assembling his kit and readying it for departure. Yet he was still standing there, motionless, when the buzzer at his door sounded some time later.

He blinked back to awareness, more disgusted with himself than ever, and growled, *"Come."*

Spinning on his heel to face the room's entrance, he was surprised when the door slid open to reveal the summer-blue gaze, fine-boned features, and spun-gold hair that had been playing behind his eyes like a holovid as he stared into space. She stood, hesitating at the threshold, her spine held straight as if girding herself for battle.

"Ash told me what a *seelaht* is," she said, without preamble. "If that's the best way for me to accompany you while you meet with this Jago person, then I think we should do it."

He stared at her, taking in the dull flatness behind her eyes and the pale cast of her skin.

"No," he said without thought.

She looked at him without expression. "Why not?"

Why not, indeed? There was the real reason, and the reason he was willing to give her. "You would be humiliating yourself. Pretending to be a—" He paused, searching his vocabulary. "I do not know the right word in Human Standard."

"Sex slave," she supplied, still without any spark of emotion.

Hunter frowned. "You would be subject to all manner of degradation from those we are likely to meet. If you broke character, it would mean certain death… or worse."

She didn't even blink. "Countless lives depend on what I do in the coming days. I'm standing here, alive and breathing, when I should be dead a dozen times over. I'm completely reliant on a group of people whom I've been told over and over have no decency or conscience—who would rape, torture, and kill me without a second thought."

Her brow furrowed. "But you haven't. Either this is some elaborate game to you, and you'll turn on me at some random moment, or it's not, and you really are risking your lives to help me. Whatever the case, nothing that's likely to happen if I pretend to be your human sex toy could be any worse than what I *expected* to happen when I woke up here and realized who you were."

She was, he realized, still in shock—running on autopilot after tumbling into a situation far beyond her ability to cope with. And yet, she had acted honorably and intelligently throughout—even when she was obviously panicked. First, in attempting to hide and protect her secret when she had reason to believe that she was in the hands of the enemy, and later, doing everything possible to assist them when it turned out she was not.

How many Vithii civilians would have acted as bravely? Fates above, she was an *accountant*, of all things. Her turncoat father should be whipped for putting her in such an impossible position in the first place.

"Do you truly understand what you would be agreeing to?" he asked, knowing that he was wavering and hating himself for it.

Her lips twisted in something too bitter to be called a smile. "Ash didn't pull any punches, and he seemed to know what he was talking about. But it still sounded like all that's required on my end is to show a lot of skin, hang all over you, and look suitably vacuous. I expect I can manage those three things well enough."

Hunter wondered how well *he* was likely to manage the first two items on that list.

"And did Ash mention the collar?" he asked, aware that he sounded belligerent.

"Yes," she answered dully. When he didn't respond, she blinked large blue eyes up at him. "The human population of Ilarius is going to *die*. What does it matter? What does *anything* that I have to do to stop it *matter*?"

The answer was that it didn't. Except inasmuch as it did.

"I may not be able to keep you safe," he said.

The look she gave him was almost pitying. "I'm Zarian Chantrell's daughter," she said. "Right now, *no one* can keep me safe."

A complicated knot seemed to settle in Hunter's chest. "Be ready to leave in two cycles." The words emerged sounding cold. "You'll travel in the courier ship with Ash and Ryder."

She nodded, accepting the chill distance behind the command with the same impassivity she'd accepted everything else. When she had gone, Hunter allowed himself to slump, just the tiniest bit, one hand reaching out to rest on the frame of the bare cot he slept on. A choked, pain-filled whisper drifted along the edges of his memory.

Hunter. Love you, sweetheart—

Would you still love me, he wondered, *if you could see what I've become?*

SEVEN

Skye sat in the single passenger seat of Ash's stolen courier, her spine held straight and tense as Ash and Ryder bluffed their way through the first of what would be a series of communications checkpoints dotting the approach to Ilarius.

Once they had the all clear, Ash looked over his shoulder, sharing the reassuring flicker of an eyebrow. "See?" he said. "No sweat. Believe me, at this point I could run the Regime blockade in my sleep."

"What about the others?" she asked, still unable to relax. Both Kade and The Rook maintained two-seat fighters, and were approaching by different routes to avoid suspicion.

Ash's smile was tight. "Well, they'll probably need to stay awake, to be fair. But it's hardly the first time they've done it. And they're using the codes and fake registration I gave them, so it should be fine."

"Modesty has always been one of your most attractive virtues, *leetha*," Ryder muttered, not looking up from the readouts she was monitoring on the copilot's console.

"And here I thought you admired me for my dashing good looks, doc," Ash said.

Ryder tore her gaze away from the screens in front of her to shoot him a sour look. "If you keep letting Vithii perverts pummel you for entertainment, you may lose those good looks sooner rather than later, Ash."

Ash's face closed off and he turned back to his own console. "It's a calculated risk. There's more at stake here than just me."

Ryder made a noise of disgust, and the cramped cabin descended into uncomfortable silence.

Skye cleared her throat. "So, speaking of calculated risks. Is there anything else I need to know about pretending to be The Rook's *seelaht*? I'm already thanking the stars that it's summer in the Capital—for some strange reason, I seem to be feeling a bit of a draft."

The forced joke felt flat as soon as it passed her lips, but Ash graced her with a huff of dark amusement. After some discussion, he had helped her rip the hell out of her black jumpsuit. The thing had already seen a difficult few days, so it wasn't a great loss to human couture, by any stretch. Even so, Skye had felt momentarily disconcerted by the knowledge that she had no other clothes, and it was unlikely she'd be able to acquire more anytime soon.

Regardless, her plain though respectable jumpsuit was now about as far from respectable as one could get without running afoul of public indecency laws. She and Ash had cut and ripped it strategically, resulting in a sort of wild-woman-slash-space-castaway vibe that covered the important bits, and not much else. It felt completely ridiculous—not to mention embarrassing—but Ash assured her it would suffice for the job at hand.

He shot her another sideways glance. "Well, the first thing I'd do is not call him The Rook. He hates it, and not without reason. That's the sobriquet gifted to him by the Regime, not anything he ever chose. His name's Hunter. Hunter Tarthasian. Though while you're in character, you'd do best to call him *Fei'graal*, if you call him anything."

"Or, better yet," Ryder added, "keep your mouth shut and focus on staying alive."

Skye knew, intellectually, that all of this should be making far more of an impact on her than it was. But, despite the cool air raising gooseflesh on her exposed skin and the stiff plastic collar around her neck—adapted from a strap on one of the portable sensor units from Ryder's medbay—none of it felt real. None of it touched her.

"What does *Fei'graal* mean?" she asked absently.

"Master," Ash replied, and she couldn't parse the complicated tangle of bitterness and resignation that seemed to lurk beneath the word.

<hr>

"Vessel registration eight-one-seven-six-nine-two-tango-alpha, you are clear for final approach and touchdown at hangar facility two-two-three. Do not deviate from filed flight plans."

The tinny voice crackled over Hunter's comm speakers, and the tense line of muscle at the corner of his jaw softened incrementally.

Draven shifted next to him in the copilot's seat, positioning his mic to reply. "Message received," he said. "Course laid in. Try not to fall asleep down there, eh?"

The speaker crackled again. *"The Regime never sleeps,"* came the reply, but even over the low-quality commlink, the touch of weary sarcasm behind the words bled through. In the midst of totalitarian horror, low-paid grunts remained low-paid grunts the universe over, clocking in and clocking out so they could afford to go to the nearest drinking hole or whorehouse afterward and forget their sorrows for a while.

Draven clicked off the link and settled back. Hunter eased the sleek fighter through the lower atmosphere and toward one of the commercial hangars Kade maintained behind complex layers of secrecy, shell corporations, and bureaucratic red tape.

"That went well," Draven said. "Think the others had any trouble?"

Hunter shrugged, not bothering with an answer. If they had, he and Draven would find out about it soon enough. Ash's codes had never failed them yet, however.

Already, he was thinking ahead to the meeting with Jago, and what would need to come after, assuming Kade was successful in negotiating the use of a lab. There were layers upon layers of potential obstructions between them and their ultimate goal. And, as Ash had said, time was not their friend. The uncertainty of the situation pricked at him—he preferred scenarios he could better control.

Control. The image of a collar buckled snug around the pale, delicate flesh of an unprotected throat flashed before his eyes, and he quashed it with ruthless irritation. This whole thing was fucked five ways from midday, and they were going to be lucky not to end up dead or locked in a Regime torture cell by the end of it.

The hangar entrance retracted beneath them, and Hunter forced his mind back to the matter at hand. One step, then the next, then the next. That was all he could do. He just hoped it would be enough to get those he considered to be under his care through what was to come, and out the other side.

◆

A flashing purple light—the Vithii color of warning—strobed inside the huge hangar where Ash had parked the courier.

"That'll be Hunter," Ash said, relief clear in his tone despite his earlier bravado.

"With Kade right on his tail, it looks like," Ryder added, straightening up from her sensor display and turning it off. "As per usual."

Two sleek black fighters coasted down through the gaping maw in the hangar roof and settled into the spaces on either side of the courier with identical puffs of dust and steam as the landing gear touched down.

Ash swiveled his pilot's seat and turned to look at Skye, unstrapping himself from the five-point flight harness as he did. "Are you ready for this? I need to leave you, now that the others are here. I was due back quite some time ago, and these days, doing things that are unpredictable attracts far too much notice from the wrong kind of people."

I am about as far from ready for this as it's possible to be, she thought.

"Yeah, I'm good," she said. "Thanks, Ash."

Something in his expression made her think he saw more than he let on, but he only nodded and said, "All right, then." He rose and clapped Ryder on the shoulder as he made his way out of the clearsteel dome of the courier's control center. "Try to stay above room temperature, you two. I'll be in contact."

"Don't do anything stupider than usual, *leetha*," Ryder told his retreating back, and he graced them with a final, careless wave before disappearing down the ladder toward the airlock hatch. Ryder sighed.

Skye realized that she was still wearing her harness and fumbled to release it, her fingers clumsy and numb. Ryder unsnapped her own harness and stood, stretching. The medic had exchanged the practical unisex coveralls she'd worn on the lunar outpost for a sleek, form-fitting sleeveless shirt that showed off her Vithii musculature, along with tight black breeches that looked like real leather to Skye's practiced eye. Silver buckles gleamed in neat rows along the outside edge of the tall, thick-soled boots she wore.

Ass-kicking boots, offered a voice that sounded an awful lot like Temple's. Skye shivered at the unwanted reminder of her foster brother.

Her harness finally came loose, leaving her no more excuses to remain huddled in her seat.

"Come on," Ryder said, as if reading her mind. "Day's not getting any younger, and this won't be any more pleasant later than it will be right now."

Skye nodded resolutely, took a deep breath past the faint, claustrophobic constriction of the collar, and rose on shaky legs to go join her temporary *Fei'graal*.

Hunter stepped onto the gritty tarmac of the hangar floor, moving aside so Draven could follow him down the ladder from the cockpit. Ash approached them from the belly of his stolen ship and gave a quick upward jerk of the chin in greeting.

"All good?" the human asked.

Hunter shrugged in reply. "Slow day in the space lanes. The traffic control grunts were half asleep. You heading off now?"

Ash's eyes slid away, flickering over Draven's face without sticking. "Yeah. I'll be in touch, and you can reach me in the usual way if there's an emergency." He looked back to Hunter, earnest. "Be careful with the girl, Hunter. She's scared shitless. She's also still in shock, and if it all hits her at the wrong moment, it's not gonna be pretty."

Kade and Pax chose that moment to join them. "This whole thing isn't gonna be pretty, period," said Kade, with his typical sunny optimism and good cheer.

"You're the one who decided to drag Jago into the mix, Kade," Hunter pointed out. "Are you jacked and ready to go for the next little while?"

"He's good," Pax said, ignoring Kade's dark look at being talked about like he wasn't standing right there.

"I'll leave you gents to it, in that case," said Ash. "Hopefully I'll have intel for you on the water treatment plant by this time tomorrow."

Hunter nodded. "Fair winds, *leetha*. We'll keep you updated as we're able."

Ash flashed him a tight smile and ran a quick, mercurial gaze over the others before striding away toward the street-level entrance.

Movement at the corner of his eye made Hunter's hand twitch toward the blaster at his hip, his reflexes already falling into crisis mode. It was only Ryder and her human charge, though. *His* human charge, now, he corrected himself.

Fuck.

Suddenly, what she was wearing—or more accurately, what she *wasn't*—penetrated his awareness, and he stared at creamy skin revealed behind artfully torn black cloth, along with smooth-muscled legs that seemed to go on forever.

She looked like one of the slender, elegant statues from the late neoclassical period in Vithii art, brought to life. No Vithii woman ever had waves of smooth, spun-gold hair falling nearly to her waist, though, or delicate features like some mythical woodland sprite.

Hunter felt the whole ridiculous plan start to slew sideways. It was the same sensation he felt in the moments before a mission went wrong. The same sickening dip of the stomach—familiar from his misspent youth—that came from cornering too fast on a stolen hoverbike. Feeling the stabilizers grab nothing but air; knowing that you had no choice but to ride the thing down to the ground, even though the first touch of your flesh against the sandpaper grit of the road would hurt like hot knives.

Then she got close enough for him to see her expression—dazed and lost. The blank void behind her eyes brought him back to himself enough to avoid any overt reaction as she walked up to him and fit her body against his side, soft curves pressing against his hard muscles.

Now it was his turn to be dazed as a sleek form that should have been all wrong for his molded against him. She fit like the final piece of one of those old wooden puzzles his childhood guardians had been so fond of. Without conscious volition, his eyes landed on Ryder, searching for… what? Help? Some explanation for his body's betrayal?

Ryder was the polar opposite of the human woman now tucked under his shoulder. She was dressed to intimidate—hard, cold, and bristling with weapons—everything carefully calculated to remind any Vithii male who came near her of the deadliness of an unreceptive female of the species. She stared back at him impassively, no doubt seeing more than he wanted her to see.

He realized that the silence around them had stretched for an unnaturally long time.

"So," Pax said, breaking it with his usual lack of interest in meatbag emotional minutiae, "are we doing this, or what?"

"'Course we are," Kade said. "I didn't come back to this shithole for my health."

"Let's go," Hunter said, the words emerging deep and rough. He eased away from the human so he could look down at her. Blank blue eyes stared back at his. "Walk a step or two behind me. Keep your eyes down. Don't get too close to the others' personal space—not even Ryder's. No matter what happens, don't break character. Doing so could be fatal, and not just for you."

She nodded and immediately looked down at her feet.

Something compelled him to add, "I'll do my best to keep you from harm. So will the others."

She did not respond, but whether it was because she was already acting in character or because she didn't believe him, he had no idea. With nothing else to do, he led the way out of the hangar, into the tense, stifling atmosphere of the Capital.

Kade had long ago ensured that the security cameras in and around the hangars he owned transmitted only innocuous doctored video of normal comings and goings. In addition, Hunter knew Kade carried a jammer that would interfere with image quality on nearby cameras that were outside of his direct control. Of course, the pattern of technical glitches as they moved was its own sort of giveaway, but someone would have to be looking for it.

Night was falling. Everything was gray. Gray buildings, gray pavement, gray smog in the sky giving way to the heavy slate color that was as close to darkness as a city with this many lights ever got. The stink of people—Vithii and human—mixed with the smells of pollution, garbage, and cooking food to form a dense miasma that clung to the skin.

Public transit was not an option, so they strode through the bustling streets of the lower east side openly, nervous civvies crossing the road to avoid them—scurrying out of their way at the first whiff of the danger that surrounded their black-clad group like an aura.

As they moved deeper into Vithii gang territory, the character of the area changed, auto-launderettes and convenience stores giving way to gambling dens, clubs, and whorehouses. The smell of piss and vomit wafted from dark alleyways as they passed. The civvies became fewer and farther between, replaced by addicts, thrill-seekers, and dead-eyed prostitutes. Hulking Vithii lookouts watched them from the shadows.

Hunter knew well enough that Jago would have been informed of their approach as soon as they passed into his territory. They were more or less at the bastard's mercy, a fact that ate at Hunter's stomach lining like cheap, home-brewed rotgut. The only saving grace was that calling the authorities on them would also bring those same authorities down on *him*.

Unless, of course, he had the city's security forces in his pocket—bought and paid for. Which was certainly a possibility.

Hunter kept part of his attention on their surroundings and part of it on the woman walking a step behind his left shoulder. He was painfully aware of the way the goons watching them raked greedy eyes over her. So was she, even with her eyes locked on the ground beneath her feet—he could smell her fear. Sad to say, such a reaction was not at all out of character for a human *seelaht*, but it pressed his spine straight and his chest out, nonetheless—muscles tense and bulging as instinct propelled him to make himself as big and threatening as possible.

It will serve, he thought. *It may even prove a benefit.*

If he could convince himself of that, it might supplant his growing sense of dismay at the degree to which his mating instincts were rising, trying to take over.

Kade led them to Impulse, the exclusive nightclub at the heart of Jago's little empire, where he could often be found holding court.

"*Impulse*," Ryder muttered, a sneer sliding across her strong features. "The only *impulse* I ever experience in this snake pit is the urge to perform an unplanned bilateral orchiectomy on some mouth-breathing fashion victim with an attitude."

Hunter could certainly sympathize. He was more than content to let Kade take the lead with the club's owner, since it would be more difficult to control his desire to rip the bastard's lungs out if he had to speak with the greasy fucker directly.

Still in the lead, Kade walked past the line of outrageously dressed hopefuls waiting to see if they would make the cut for admittance tonight. Hunter and the others followed him, ignoring the chorus of voices raised in outrage as one might ignore an insect's buzz.

The bouncer was large, stony-faced, and well armed. Pax could, no doubt, have taken him down in seconds—but that would not be in line with their agenda here. Kade fetched up in front of the man.

"Back of the line, or I start removing body parts," said the bouncer, with the sort of confidence that meant he must have backup just inside the door.

"We're here by request," Kade replied, visibly unimpressed. "*Birds of a feather.*"

Behind Hunter, Skye let out a nearly inaudible choked noise, but when he glanced at her, she was blank-faced, staring down at the ground, the picture of meek docility. The bouncer showed no sign of having noticed the lapse. His eyes raked over the group, lingering for a moment on Hunter's tattoos before he jerked his head toward the door.

"Go in. The boys'll take you down to the lower level. The boss is waiting for you there."

Kade nodded and brushed past him. The rest of them followed, to jeers of discontent from those waiting in the queue. The inside of the club was like a womb—blood-warm, humid, and done up in deep shades of red and black. Even near the entryway, the pulse of bass was an insistent, primal heartbeat, echoing in the space beneath the ribs. The air was thick with the fumes of drugs, both natural and synthetic.

The *boys* were lounging in an alcove off the narrow hallway that led from the outside door to the club's interior. They looked up with interest, taking in Hunter's group with eyes that turned greedy upon seeing Ryder and Skye. Hunter felt his hackles rise, a growl trying to rumble its way out of his chest.

"Well, now, what's all this?" said the tallest of the four.

"Take us to Jago," Kade ordered, in the bored tone of one used to being obeyed. "We're expected."

"Are you, now?" the grunt said smoothly. "Well, I guess you'd better go with my friend Lash, here." He jerked his chin toward the guard propped against the wall next to him. "Why don't you leave your females with us? We'll show 'em a good time while you talk business with the boss."

EIGHT

The man grinned and sauntered forward, smooth as a jungle predator, until he was face to face with Ryder. He lifted a hand as if to stroke her face. At the same time, two of the remaining three approached Skye.

Without conscious thought, Hunter intercepted the closest one and grabbed his wrist, dislocating his thumb with a smooth, almost careless movement. Before the howl of pain had torn its way free from the guard's throat, Hunter had a hand wrapped around the second one's neck, fingertips pressing against the main artery running to his brain in clear warning.

When the dull red haze cleared from Hunter's vision, he became aware of Ryder, who had a small, wicked looking dagger pressed to the first male's crotch. His hand was frozen in the air, the movement toward her face arrested as she grinned at him, showing teeth.

"You know, it's been nearly two weeks since I last castrated a horny stray dog," she said pleasantly. "I'd hate to think I was getting out of practice."

Kade walked up, the picture of arrogance, and moved the man's hand down to his side with the careless press of an index finger. When that was done, he moved Ryder's knife hand the same way, and gave the frozen grunt a sharp smile and a companionable pat on the shoulder.

"The *females* will be coming with us, as I'm sure you have gathered by now," he said, ignoring the pained groans coming from the guard trying to jam his thumb back into its socket, as well as the choked noises coming from the one Hunter was half-strangling. "Lash, was that your name? Perhaps you'd care to lead the way?"

Lash looked at the guard who'd annoyed Ryder—the apparent leader. The man was obviously seething, but he gave a single, tight nod, just as obviously unwilling to risk his boss's wrath by tangling with people Jago had arranged to meet.

Hunter let the man whose throat he was squeezing drop, ignoring him as he staggered to the nearest wall to support himself, clutching his abused neck. Lash gave them all wary looks, but headed deeper into the building without a word, clearly expecting them to follow.

They did, without comment.

After the surge of instinctive male protectiveness, Hunter's senses were so closely attuned to Skye that he could feel her trembling even without physical contact. Ignoring his earlier instructions to her about staying behind him, he dropped back a pace and gathered her against his side with one arm. Her skin was cold to the touch despite the too-warm atmosphere of the club. Little bursts of shivers wracked her slender frame, growing further apart and of shorter duration as they walked.

That's it, he urged silently. *Be strong, little sparrow. Don't lose your nerve now. Not here. Not yet. Not when you've already come so far.*

Skye pressed her body to The Rook's. No, to *Hunter's*. She needed to remember not to think of him that way—it was the least she could do, given what he and his friends were risking for her.

She tried to make it look as if she were fawning over him, and not like her knees were about to give out. He had surprised her, dropping back to take her under his wing, so to speak. He had also surprised her with the speed and viciousness of his attack on the two guards who had come at her like wolves after a defenseless lamb.

Perhaps she shouldn't have been surprised, though. Just because he apparently wasn't what the Regime said he was, didn't mean he wasn't dangerous. Quite the opposite, really. If he weren't dangerous, the Regime would have no reason to fear him.

He had moved like a predator. Efficient. Ruthless. Merciless. He had acted almost before she had time to begin panicking, though that hadn't kept reaction from setting in once she understood what might easily have happened to her.

Part of her envied Ryder—armed, confident, and deadly. Ryder didn't need to be rescued. She didn't need to be protected. But that was unfair. Ryder had only been dealing with a single Vithii. If she'd been outnumbered, if she'd needed help, Skye was quickly coming to understand that Kade, Pax, and the others would have ripped her opponents limb from limb to keep her safe.

Still, there had been something almost... *primal*... in the way Hunter had defended Skye from the two guards. As if it was personal. Which didn't make any sense. Why would he care, beyond a general feeling of responsibility for her after dragging her to this place, collared like a dog? Though that wasn't fair, either. She'd volunteered for this. In fact, she'd had to talk him into it.

Even so, he'd been quite clear—his interest was in taking down the Regime. Nothing else. None of which explained the strong arm currently wrapped around her in a protective embrace. Or the fact that, for whatever reason, that embrace *did* seem to be helping keep her panic at bay.

Perhaps, she thought, the contact was not so much *protective* as *possessive*. Part of the act. Despite Ash's coaching, she was far from an expert on the Vithii etiquette involved with keeping a human sex slave.

It didn't matter. The important part was, she had calmed down enough that she wasn't in danger of puking, or fainting, or otherwise doing something to blow their cover. Which was just as well, since they seemed to be approaching their destination. They entered a mirrored lift, which went down a level and disgorged them into a corridor decorated more like an expensive five-star hotel than a club. She could hear the rumble of rough voices ahead, and the walls seemed to pulse with the Vithii techno-dub coming from upstairs.

With her eyes on the floor beneath her scuffed black ankle boots, she could only take in her surroundings in tiny glimpses—an upward glance from beneath her eyelashes, a blurred impression from her peripheral vision. Since she had left the hangar, footwear had somehow become more of a personal identifier to her than faces.

As they walked toward the voices, Hunter removed his arm. Without a word, she inserted herself once more behind his left shoulder, following him and trying not to draw attention. The others surrounded her in a loose cluster, as if forming an irregular barrier between her and her surroundings. She wondered if it was intentional.

Even if it wasn't, she still appreciated it.

They entered the room where Jago was presumably entertaining his guests. The shiny flooring that might or might not have been real marble gave way to a thick carpet which had once been luxurious, but was now showing signs of wear. A quick glance revealed a tableau that put her in mind of pictures of the lost mural by da Vinci, depicting the old religious event called the Last Supper.

Now, though, the figure at the center of the table was not Christ, but rather the fattest Vithii Skye had ever seen. She immediately looked down again, unwilling to risk getting caught staring. Was this Jago?

The question was answered almost immediately when the guard strode up to him and said, "Visitors for you, Boss. They say they're expected."

"And so they are," said a smooth voice, the tone almost oily. "Sit down, sit down. Kade, my *friend*, it's been a long time. Though perhaps I should bill you for damaging two of my guards on your way in."

"If your guard is rendered useless by a simple dislocated thumb, it sounds like what you really need are better guards," Kade said, pleasantly enough.

Chair legs dragged across the faded carpet, and she realized that there wasn't a seat available for her. She had the same ridiculous feeling of being caught out that she used to have as a child playing musical chairs at school. She froze, unsure what to do.

Gentle downward pressure on her forearm further confused her, until she realized with a flush that Hunter was guiding her to kneel at his feet. She swallowed the unexpected spark of surprise and humiliation and awkwardly arranged herself on the floor, trying to ignore the crumbs of food and bits of dirt or gods-knew-what under her bare knees.

None of this mattered.

She'd apparently been too slow. Too unpracticed. She'd drawn attention—she could feel eyes on her, even if she didn't dare look up to confirm it.

"New pet, Hunter?" Jago's sibilant voice asked. "I didn't realize you were in the market. If I had, I could have sold you something a bit better trained. Where did you find this one, anyway?"

Skye couldn't help the blood that rose to her cheeks.

"I have my sources," Hunter said, his tone giving nothing away.

Jago made a considering noise. "And, while we're on the subject, what *is* that abomination around its neck? Mother of the prophets—if nothing else, I can at least sell you a decent collar while you're here."

Despite her intention not to let any of this touch her, Skye's ears burned with a potent mix of anger and indignity at being discussed like an object. Like *property*.

"She hasn't earned it yet," Hunter was saying, and perhaps Skye imagined the undertone of ire hidden beneath his completely flat voice.

There was a beat of silence before their host laughed, loud and deep. "It always was difficult to take your measure, Hunter," he said. "You're an inscrutable one, and no mistake. But you didn't come here to talk about your new *seelaht*. Kade, your communiqué intrigued me. Have a drink, and we'll discuss things.

Unfortunately, *things* seemed to encompass every-thing *but* the use of the lab. Jago steered the conversation to gossip, reminiscences, and stories about his recent business exploits for what felt like *forever*.

And Skye wasn't the only one getting increas-ingly restive, she could tell. Hunter's body was growing tense and drawn in his chair next to her. She could feel his restlessness grow with each new round of drinks or food, each new toast. There was an undercurrent here that she hadn't fully grasped, she knew.

It also didn't help that she was still weak from the shuttle crash, her physical reserves depleted. After the first couple of cycles, it became more and more difficult to ignore her growing hunger and thirst in the presence of so much rich food and drink.

In an attempt to distract both of them, and for a lack of any other ideas, she leaned sideways against the rigid muscles of Hunter's leg, wrapping an arm around his calf and letting her cheek rest on his knee. She felt him go absolutely still for a mo-ment before he consciously relaxed his tense posture.

A large, callused hand came to rest on her head, smoothing her hair back like an indulgent owner stroking a cat's ears. Despite the circumstances, she couldn't suppress the faint shiver that traveled down her spine at the unexpected intimacy of the touch. No one had touched her like that in… how long had it even *been*? She honestly couldn't remember.

A moment later, the hand trailed down to her chin, tilting her face up toward his. She took this as permission to look up at him, and watched the faint furrow of his heavy brow as he studied her features. She knew she must look awful—pale and wan. When he released the gentle grip, she looked down again demurely. A moment later, a metal goblet of something—probably wine, from the smell—appeared in her field of vision.

She almost reached up to grasp it before stopping herself. It didn't take a genius to figure out that such a gesture would be out of place for the role she was playing. Another blush colored her cheeks, but she meekly allowed him to position the cup at her lips and tip it up until she could drink with careful sips.

Food followed—small tidbits transferred directly from his fingers to her lips. There was something simultaneously bizarre and oddly profound about being hand-fed like this by a man on whom she was utterly reliant for her continued safety, while trapped deep in hostile and unfamiliar territory.

It was a shock when she first noticed the fine tremor in his fingertips. It was nearly undetectable, but she was confident she wasn't imagining it. Was this affecting him as well? Why? On a hunch, she wrapped her lips around his fingers for a moment longer than necessary, laving juice from the slice of hydroponically grown fruit off the pads with her tongue. She risked a glance up at him as she was doing it, catching a flash of… *something* behind his clear green eyes.

What the hell?

They must *both* be losing their minds under the strain. Taken aback, she drew away enough to indicate that she wasn't hungry any more, and he let her. The next time she snuck a glance at him, his mask was firmly back in place.

The meeting dragged on. And on. And *on*. Then, something in Kade's voice drew her attention away from her boredom and aching knees. He sounded… shaky. Ill, perhaps. A jolt of worry shot through her. From what she had seen of him, Kade was molded from tempered durasteel. What would make him sound like that?

Hunter had tensed as well, one hand clenched on his muscular thigh. Kade was seated off to Skye's right side, within her line of sight even though the table hid most of the others from her vantage point. She peeked at him from under her eyelashes, alarmed at the pale cast of his face and the beads of sweat visible on his forehead.

She glanced at Hunter to see his reaction, and found a muscle working in the corner of his jaw. Disquiet churned in her gut.

Jago continued to talk and laugh as if unaware of any problem, though surely he could not fail to miss the uncharacteristic weakness in Kade's voice. After another tortuous few minutes, Hunter slammed a palm down on the table, making Skye jump.

"Enough, Jago," he said, his anger clear. "You have heard our terms and proposal. What is your answer?"

Skye could hear the slow smile behind Jago's words as he answered. She loathed it, even though she still didn't truly understand what was happening between Kade, Hunter, and their slimy host.

"Easy now, my friend. There is no call for such theatrics. You had only to say so if you did not wish to continue enjoying my hospitality." He paused deliberately. "Now, perhaps you could remind me once more of the details?"

Hunter was practically vibrating with anger as Kade reiterated their proposed terms in a shaky voice. Each word seemed to be an effort that threatened to strip his throat raw, and again, Skye wondered with real fear what was happening to him. When he subsided, his rasping breathing audible to everyone at the table, Jago laughed.

"Yes, that all sounds quite reasonable," he said. "Give me your ship's transceiver codes and I'll arrange access to the lab for you first thing in the morning."

Beneath her hands, Hunter was still trembling with suppressed rage. She tightened her grip, trying to keep him from doing anything that might jeopardize what they had just apparently achieved.

"Now, would you all care for some dessert?" Jago asked, wicked glee hiding under a thin facade of innocence.

"No," Hunter growled. "We would not. We're leaving now."

He scraped his heavy chair back and rose, Skye scrambling to follow him on legs that pricked with pins and needles after so long in an uncomfortable, cramped position. From the corner of her eye, she saw Kade stagger a bit as he tried to stand. Ryder made a move toward him, only to stop when he growled a warning at her and locked his knees, steadying himself. Tension was thick around the little group as they left the banquet room and returned to the lift.

They were not escorted this time, and Skye looked up with worried eyes as Hunter tried to take Kade's arm, only to have his hand shaken off roughly.

"*Cameras*," Kade ground out.

There was a brief pause, before Hunter said, "Idiot," in a tone that was oddly soft.

Not sure if the camera remark had been directed at her or not, Skye forced her gaze back down, just in case. The walk back to the entrance seemed to take forever. As they passed the alcove, Skye recognized the boots of the guard who had tried to threaten Ryder. He was holding a stiletto in one hand, twirling the blade through his fingers, back and forth… back and forth.

Skye shuddered, but neither the guard nor the bouncer at the door tried to stop them as they spilled back onto the street—empty now of would-be club attendees. Only when they were away from the circle of weak light illuminating the front of the club did Kade allow Hunter to shove a shoulder under his and sling an arm around him, supporting him as he sagged.

NINE

Skye held her breath as Hunter hustled Kade into the first stinking, deserted alley they came to and propped him against the stained plasticrete wall. Kade's harsh panting echoed around the dark space.

"Pax," Hunter hissed, and a moment later, a beam of actinic white light from the cyborg's facial implant illuminated Kade's pale, sweating face.

Kade winced, half raising a shaking hand as if to fend off the glare.

"Where is it?" Hunter asked, the words still tight with anger.

"Inner p-pocket," Kade managed, giving up and screwing his eyes shut to block out the light.

Hunter rummaged inside Kade's black leather jacket and pulled out a shiny little hypo-injector. He glanced at it to check the dosage and jabbed it into Kade's neck without ceremony. Kade jerked and shuddered, Hunter's renewed grip on his shoulders all that was keeping him upright.

"Will he be all right? What's wrong with him?" Skye asked, her own voice none too steady.

Ryder came up, tilting Kade's head back and peeling up one eyelid to peer at his pupil.

"He's a neurotonin addict," she said absently. "The onset of withdrawal symptoms begins four to six cycles after the last effective dose."

"Shut up, Ryder. What the fuck happened to doctor-patient confidentiality?" Kade ground out, the words sounding like broken glass.

Ryder shrugged. "I was disbarred. Don't have to worry about that kind of shit any more, do I?"

Skye suddenly remembered Ryder asking Kade if he was due for an injection, back when she'd been stuck in the medbay on the lunar outpost, and things started to fall into place. But... "If you had the injection with you, why didn't you just go to the lav and use it?"

"Because he's an idiot," Hunter said.

"Because I wouldn't give that slimy bastard the satisfaction," Kade said, sounding a bit more like himself.

"Whereas this is *ever* so much more dignified," Ryder put in.

"It's the principle of the thing," Kade muttered.

"So Jago was keeping us there on purpose?" Skye asked, trying to understand.

"His little joke," Kade said bitterly.

"Kade outmaneuvered him in a business deal a few years back," Hunter said. "Jago takes his petty revenge wherever he can get it."

Skye shook her head. "But... wouldn't it have been better revenge to deny us use of the lab? He agreed just like that! Like it was nothing!"

"Of course he did," Kade said, letting his head rest against the wall behind him, eyes closed in obvious exhaustion. "Money trumps revenge, every time. But this way, he gets both." He sneered. "Everybody's happy. *Win-win*."

She didn't know what to say to that. Perhaps there was nothing to say. They had access to the lab, and Kade would apparently be all right now that he'd gotten his fix.

"Not everybody's happy," she said eventually. "I'm sorry you had to go through that."

He opened cold gray eyes to glare at her. "I don't need your pity."

As if the burst of anger toward her had somehow lent him strength, he batted Hunter's hands away and pushed off of the wall, taking his own weight before he spoke again.

"I couldn't arrange for a reliable safehouse on such short notice. We'll have to kip in the hangar," he said, clearly wanting to move onto a different subject. "We should probably take it in shifts to keep watch tonight, just in case."

"Of course," Hunter said. "I assume we'll have the place to ourselves?"

Kade nodded. "I had all of the employees sent home. The manager told them the place was getting fumigated for vermin. We won't be bothered."

"Except by the vermin," Ryder muttered.

"I can book you a room in one of Jago's hotels if you'd rather," Kade shot back. Ryder only snorted.

By silent accord, the six of them exited the alley, Kade's shoulders bowed in obvious exhaustion despite his attempt to put up a strong front. Remembering herself, Skye lowered her eyes again, playing her part with renewed determination now that they were so close to their goal.

The walk back to the hangar was without mishap, and Skye sighed with relief when the door closed behind them, shutting out the dangerous, stinking city beyond. Kade enabled multiple layers of locking codes behind them, sealing them in and everything else out. As if the final beep of confirmation was some sort of signal, her fingers scrabbled of their own accord at the plastic collar buckled around her neck. She practically tore it off, throwing it aside with unexpected force.

"Don't lose that," Hunter said. "We'll need it again tomorrow."

She nodded without meeting his eyes, attempting to contain her sudden surge of irrational panic at having a whole night ahead of her to do nothing but think, and try not to remember the things she was purposely shoving aside.

"Where do we sleep?" she asked.

"You and Ryder can sleep on the courier," Kade said, still sounding like he needed a good night of rest himself. "The four of us will take the employee break room."

"I'll keep watch," Pax said in that flat, mechanical voice. "No need for shifts."

Hunter looked at the cyborg with an assessing gaze. "Don't drain your reserves. We may have need of them over the coming days."

Pax shrugged. "I'll power down partially and keep only the senses I need online. It's not a drain worth mentioning."

"Very well," Hunter agreed.

"Draven," Ryder said, "go get me a selection of whatever food and drink looks least unhealthy from the vend-o-mat. My patient needs to keep her strength up. Kade, you should eat something, too."

Kade grunted some sort of vague non-answer and turned to follow Draven through the nondescript door at the corner of the open hangar space. Pax crossed to Kade's fighter and climbed up to the cockpit, where he could presumably utilize the craft's sensors to keep watch in addition to whatever native systems had been installed directly into his brain.

When Draven returned with a selection of snack food and some kind of canned tea, Ryder took it and led Skye back to Ash's stolen ship. Skye glanced over her shoulder as she climbed into the airlock after the Vithii woman, only to see Hunter watching the two of them as if to make sure they were safely settled before joining the others.

A strange tightness rose in her throat and she swallowed hard to clear it. No doubt he just wanted to make sure Ryder had the correct locking codes to get them on board in Ash's absence.

She let Ryder bully her into eating and drinking, and then she sat down next to the medic, who was occupying the co-pilot's seat. The pilot's chair rocked back almost enough to be comfortable for sleeping, but not quite. Skye scooted around until she could curl sideways in it, and tried to clear her mind of all the things she could not afford to dwell on right now.

Not now. Not yet.

Even so, the best she could manage was a few minutes of light dozing here and there, punctuated by extended stretches spent staring at the tiny green and blue status lights on the panel above her, while exhaustion dragged at her like slow torture.

It was a long, long time until morning.

Her insomnia was finally interrupted by a shrill beep from the communications console. Ryder jerked into full wakefulness in an instant—doubtless a holdover from her days as a doctor—and slapped the switch.

"What?" she demanded, as Skye fumbled to return her seat to its upright position.

"It's Pax," came the tinny reply. "Jago just transmitted the details of our access to the lab, as promised. He's sending a hovercar for us shortly. Keep an eye on things while I go get the others."

"Will do," said Ryder, and switched off the comms. "Did you catch that?"

"Yeah," Skye said, and stretched cautiously in the confined space of the control center. The smell of her own stale sweat assailed her, and she wrinkled her nose. "Is there anyplace I can wash?"

"There are sinks in the employee lav," she said. "That's about it. The laboratory will have a shower facility, though."

That made sense. The labs where her father worked had always included a shower for emergency decontamination. Her breath caught in her chest at the memory of her father hunched over a microscope, intent on his work, doing what he loved best. She shoved the image aside before she could be drawn any further in that direction.

Not now. Not yet.

"Right," she said, clearing her throat when the word emerged as a croak. "Sink, it is. Hopefully one free of mysterious green sludge that cannot be killed by conventional means."

A short time later, she was once again standing behind Hunter, collar in place and eyes cast downward, as Jago's hovercar arrived for them. The thing was huge and posh. The driver, silent and respectful. As best she could tell, the lab was located clear on the other side of the city from the hangar. She wondered if they would pass close to her apartment in the Capital's lower district, or the zoo where Temple had met with her and first told her about what their father had done, plunging her life into chaos in the space of five minutes.

Again, she made herself think of something else. *Anything* else. Not Temple. Not her father.

Instead, she speculated on how much Kade must have paid for unrestricted use of the lab. If she asked, would he tell her? She doubted it. It must have been a fortune, though, in exchange for the kind of service and cooperation they seemed to be getting from his old rival Jago.

The luxurious hovercar stopped at every Regime checkpoint, only to be waved through without a fuss when they reached the front of the queue. The tinted windows hid them from outside view, and not a single guard demanded to check the identity of the passengers. What kind of connection did Jago *have* with the Regime, anyway? Did he simply pay someone in the government and receive amnesty from investigation in return? Had things in the Capital truly grown that corrupt?

She huffed out a breath. Clearly they had. Given what the Premiere was planning, perhaps it shouldn't have come as a surprise to her that he had no problem consorting with criminals.

Not, she reflected, that she had much room to talk on that point. The Premiere would probably change his tune if he knew whom *else* Jago was doing business with.

When they finally arrived at their destination, the huge, underground laboratory was deserted and pristine, everything powered down except for the emergency lighting. Hunter led the way inside and started up the main systems, throwing everything into sharp, white relief as bright lights flared into life above them, one by one. Behind her, the others began unloading the things they'd brought with them from the back of the hovercar. Data files, canisters of raw materials, and Ryder's ever-growing colony of nanobots.

Everything a mad scientist needs, she thought, suppressing another sharp pang.

It was getting harder and harder not to let thoughts of what had happened at the compound where her father had been held intrude into the present. She felt shaky and disconnected from her surroundings. Queasy. She needed something to do.

"Tell me how I can help," she said.

"Quiet, *seelaht*," Hunter told her sharply, and she frowned. His eyes rested very obviously on the plastic collar, and her frown deepened. *What the hell?*

Kade was rummaging through one of the crates they'd brought. He came up a few moments later with a compact device in a smooth, oblong case, with a tiny control panel on top. His large fingers tapped at the miniaturized controls and the device hummed quietly, running up and down through a range of tones until it gave a sharp beep and went quiet.

"That should take care of the main lab," Kade said.

Skye's perplexed gaze moved from him, back to Hunter.

"Surveillance cameras," Hunter said. "You don't think Jago leaves his labs unsupervised, do you?"

Feeling suddenly stupid, she said, "Oh, right. I guess he wouldn't." Something else occurred to her. "But… won't he find it suspicious if we're jamming the signal?"

Draven snorted. "I think he'd find it more suspicious if we *weren't* jamming the signal."

"Privacy is part of what we're paying him for," Kade added dismissively.

"So… I can stop playing the *seelaht* now?" she asked.

"Yes," Hunter said. "In here, at least. I'll go disable the cameras in the rest of the compound. Sorry to snap at you."

The apology surprised her. It was obvious that he had merely been trying to keep suspicion away from her. She waved the words away, feeling the cold numbness surround her once more. "It doesn't matter."

He gave her a long look, and then went to sweep for the rest of the cameras without a word.

She took a deep breath, already beset once again by restlessness. "Seriously, though, is there anything I can do?"

Draven had pity on her. "Help me unpack the raw materials and do an inventory of what Jago left us to work with," he said. "Don't touch any of the nanotech, though—leave it for Pax and Ryder. That shit makes me nervous as fuck."

"Thanks," Pax said, deadpan.

"You know what I mean," Draven said. "C'mon, do you really *want* us messing with it when we don't know what we're doing?"

It was Ryder who answered. "No, we do not want you messing with it when you don't know what you're doing. I'm not particularly thrilled about messing with it when I *do* know what I'm doing." She shot a glance at the cyborg and shrugged. "Sorry, Pax."

Pax stared at them with an indecipherable expression and went to retrieve the nanotech himself.

Skye threw herself into unpacking and taking inventory with something akin to desperation, helping with anything the others were willing to let her do. Hunter returned as they were finishing with the last of the boxes. She could feel his eyes on her, but she did not look at him to try and gauge his expression.

"Is there anything else?" she asked instead.

"No, I think that's it," Draven said. "What's the rest of the place like, Hunter?"

"Looks like the cooks stayed here for days or weeks at a time while they were working," Hunter said. "There are sleeping rooms, bathing facilities, and a basic kitchenette stocked with Redi-meals. At least we'll be comfortable while we're trying to save the world."

Skye absolutely did not want to think about sleeping, and eating, and all of the other things that one did when one had nothing else that needed doing.

"So, what next?" she asked. "What do we do now?"

"*We* start work on synthesizing the precursors for your sire's formula," Ryder said. "*You* go eat something and get more rest, because you're still weak and you look like you barely slept last night."

The feeling in Skye's chest was suspiciously close to panic. "No, really," she said. "I'm fine. I can help—"

Ryder raised an eyebrow at her. "Can you? And what sort of background do you have in organic chemistry and microbiology?"

The panic crept higher. "Well… none, really. But I did grow up around labs. I could—"

Ryder cut her off. "You can rest. And eat. You're untrained, and you're exhausted. The last thing we need is someone making a mistake that costs time or creates something dangerous. Especially with bots involved."

TEN

Skye's mouth opened to argue more—to lash out at Ryder for acting like a doctor when she kept insisting she wasn't one. She caught the words in the instant before they escaped her mouth. Words meant to hurt, to strike out against her only allies. She clamped her lips shut, choking them off just in time, and made herself take what Ryder had said on board.

She was exhausted. She was upset. If she made a mistake because of her current physical or mental condition, she would not be the one who paid the price. It would be the tens of thousands of innocent humans living in the Capital, paying with their lives.

"All right," she said instead. "I couldn't possibly sleep right now, though. I'll, uh, go get some food and hang out here in case anyone needs a go-fer. Does anyone else want a Redi-meal or a drink?"

"A double whisky would be good," Kade said in an absolutely flat voice.

"He's joking," Draven said into the awkward silence that followed.

"No," Kade said. "I wasn't."

Skye was pretty sure that neurotonin addicts weren't supposed to drink alcohol for fear of trashing their brain chemistry worse than it already was. She kept quiet.

Draven spoke again. "If Jago runs this place anything like the operations where I worked growing up, there won't be any booze here, anyway. We had to wait for our off-shift days to get plastered." His gold-flecked eyes flicked to Skye. "I'll take water and whatever flavor of Redi-meal we have the most of, if you're offering."

"Sure," she said.

The others placed their simple orders as well, though Pax's included *any vegetable-based oil you can find, and sugar or a simple starch if they have it*. Hunter only shook his head in the negative, still watching her too closely for comfort.

She prepped the Redi-meals and found drinks for everyone who had requested them. There were sugar packets in a cupboard next to a canister with various kinds of tea and a powdered mix for tangy Vitharan *edelveen*. She couldn't find any oil, though, and had to run back to tell Pax. The cyborg shrugged a brawny shoulder and asked her to bring him four meal packets instead.

When everyone except Hunter was settled at an out-of-the-way workbench, eating, she retreated to the chair she'd brought in and set in a corner where it wouldn't be in anyone's way.

The reconstituted food threatened to lodge in her esophagus with every swallow, and trying to wash it down with tea just made her stomach churn. She was still picking at the congealing mess long after the others finished efficiently gulping down the basic rations. They were already back to discussing what needed to be done, Ryder, Pax, and Draven throwing around words that Skye felt she should have been able to understand after a childhood spent growing up with scientists, but couldn't.

Why didn't you pay more attention when you had the chance, she berated herself. *You could have learned enough about science to keep you from being a complete waste of space when it really mattered.*

She set the uneaten food aside on the floor next to her. Surely she could at least wash glassware for them later. Running an autoclave wasn't exactly brain surgery. She would watch and listen until it looked like those kinds of basic skills were needed, and then offer again. She needed to keep her shit together. Her heart was still racing, fast and thready, even though this was probably the safest she'd been since before she and Temple met with their fa—

Since… before the shuttle crash.

She realized with a small jolt of surprise that she had wrapped her arms around herself without noticing and was rocking forward and back in the chair with tiny movements. She was freezing, gooseflesh pebbling her skin. Was it cold in here? No, surely it was just her torn, revealing clothing. She should go and look for a lab coat she could use to cover up. They must have spare lab coats here, right?

She made herself loosen her grip around her own torso, but found that she could muster neither the energy nor the willpower to rise. The lights seemed too harsh, throwing everything into sharp relief and making her eyes water. The sound of the others' low conversation washed in and out, sometimes audible and sometimes drowned out by the rhythmic *shush-SHUSH, shush-SHUSH* of her own blood roaring in her ears.

Awareness snapped back from the dull gray fog enfolding her thoughts, and Skye realized that she must have zoned out for an extended period of time. Kade was gone—she hadn't registered him leaving—and the others were past the discussion stage and into the beakers and pipettes stage. She had been right about the existence of spare lab coats, since Draven and Ryder were now wearing them, along with nitrile gloves and safety goggles. Pax wore none of those things, obviously unconcerned by the presence of chemicals and agents that would be dangerous to the meatbags.

Hunter's absence penetrated Skye's dull wits a moment later, but before she could cast her eyes around the room to look for him, a familiar rotten-fish smell tickled at her nostrils.

———◆———

"That's pyridine, sweetheart," her father said, smiling down at her with his merry blue eyes.

"Ew," she complained, with all the distaste a nine-year-old could muster. "Why can't you use something that doesn't stink so bad?"

He laughed. "It might be stinky, but it's also useful. Sometimes nothing else will do. We use it as a precursor, and also as a solvent or a reagent."

She screwed up her face, trying to remember the important science stuff he'd been trying to teach her. "What's a reagent, Daddy?"

Before he could answer, the scene blurred and changed. Skye was older, but still felt every inch a helpless child. She and her father weren't in his lab;

they were in the dim corridors beneath the Regime's compound, leading from the research wing to the secondary hangar. There was a shuttle waiting, he'd explained. No one would expect her to steal it and flee.

Temple was gone already, drawing the guards away to keep her safe. But then a shout came from one of the cross-corridors, followed by pounding footsteps.

"Run!" her father yelled.

Skye had never heard him sound like that before. Zarian Chantrell had always been among the softest spoken of men. He didn't yell. She was already several paces ahead of him. But his shout had the opposite effect than what he'd intended. Shock tripped up Skye's feet and she stumbled to a halt, turning to see what was happening behind her.

Her father stretched a hand toward her, his mouth open as if to say something else. Before he could, a green blaster beam erupted from the side corridor and tore a smoking hole out of his chest and stomach. He spun in place under the force of the blast—a dancer's last, graceful pirouette—and his body crumpled to the ground in slow motion before her eyes.

✦

Skye tried to pull air past the obstruction lodged in her throat, vaguely aware of the ugly wheezing noise that accompanied each effort. The image of the compound was superimposed with the harsh glare of the rented lab. Neither one seemed real. Both were too terrifying to contemplate, given what they represented.

She couldn't... *breathe*... and now hulking, half-seen figures were turning, looking at her, moving toward her. Regime guards? She couldn't... couldn't let them catch her... she had to get away, she had to escape with the data files or everyone was going to die... dead... her father was *dead*—

Oh gods oh gods oh gods—

She didn't remember falling, but somehow she was on the cold floor, scrabbling backward with hands and heels like some pathetic insect, trying to get away... to get away from...

"Get back to work, you three," said a deep, calm voice from nearby—a solid point in her panicked, whirling maelstrom of awareness. "I have her. I'll deal with it."

Her vision was tunneling, gray and red and misty at the edges. She couldn't see who had spoken, but the approaching Regime guards paused, and then turned away, retreating. The deep voice had a Vithii accent. She thought she should fear it, but for some reason she latched onto it instead. Something inside her wanted—very badly—to trust that voice.

Hands touched her shoulders and she flinched, folding in on herself. A moment later, an arm like corded iron looped around her back. Strong fingers grasped her elbow, and she was lifted onto her feet like a doll that weighed nothing. Her legs might as well have been miles away—she couldn't worry about them right now with the invisible steel band growing tighter and tighter around her ribcage, suffocating her.

"Walk, or I'll carry you," said the voice. Still calm, still without emotion.

She tried to say something, but all that emerged was another panicked wheeze. Instead, she picked up first one heavy leg and then the other, over and over, though she couldn't have said if her feet were actually touching the ground. There was no feedback, no sense of being connected to her body. Only gray fog, red mist, and the terrible, terrifying constriction around her lungs that was keeping her from breathing. Had the nanobots done something to her heart? Was this—was this what a heart attack felt like?

The arm around her shifted, tucking her close to a huge, warm body. Memory dawned, followed by a flash of recognition. The club that Jago owned. *Impulse*. Hunter attacking the guards who had tried to molest her. Tucking her under his arm afterward—under The Rook's wing. A bubble of hysterical laughter stole away another fraction of her precious air.

She was growing dizzy… she needed to pass out soon… she *needed* to, because she couldn't—

"Here. Sit." The strong arms deposited her on something soft, maybe the edge of a bed. A hand between her shoulder blades urged her upper body forward and she braced her elbows on her knees, trembling violently.

"I can't… *breathe*," she forced out. It was more the shape of words than anything else. Barely even a whisper.

"Yes, you can," Hunter said. "We're planetside, and the air is plentiful here. Breathe, little sparrow, and then tell me what it is you've been hiding from, since you crashed your shuttle on our doorstep."

His hand was still on her upper back, fingers splayed, unmoving. She could feel the warmth of his body heat radiating from the point of contact, combating the icy chill that had started in her heart and crept outward until her entire body was numb and shaking. Even so, it felt like an eternity before the band around her chest shattered and she could *finally* drag in a sobbing, unhindered breath.

The air felt like tiny knives as she panted, still wanting nothing more than to pass into blissful unconsciousness, and maybe—just *maybe*—never wake up again.

But Hunter had not forgotten his earlier demand.

"Tell me now," he said, his tone uncompromising.

The words choked their way free without her permission.

"M-my f-father. Oh gods. Oh *gods*, they *killed* him… right in front of me. There was a great big h-hole in his side—"

She was rocking again, her fingers clenching the hair at her temples, pulling as if the pain could distract her somehow from the memory of— "I c-could see his bones… his organs. Charred, and smoking, like burned *meat*…" Her voice rose. "He was my *father*, and they made me watch him *die*!" Rage flooded her, swirling together with the stabbing ache of loss. "Fucking Regime *bastards*!"

A weight settled next to her, and the hand on her back that had anchored her through the storm moved to pull her into an embrace. She buried her face against Hunter's broad shoulder, breathing in the smell of musky alien sweat instead of the ghostly stench of scorched flesh.

"Then grieve him," Hunter said simply.

As if the words of permission had somehow opened the floodgates, a gasping sob wrenched at Skye's chest—ugly and primal. Another followed, and another, and another—each one tearing at her abused stomach muscles. She clutched the man holding her, fingers digging into his black shirt like claws as she tried desperately not to make too much noise.

"Come, now. Let it out, sparrow," he murmured. "You'll hurt yourself trying to hold it inside like this."

She shook her head against his solid bulk. "I can't," she choked out. "The others will hear—"

The compassion in his voice was unmistakable this time. "Have you never seen Vithii grieving? They scream their pain out to all who will listen. They howl it to the heavens. They *wail* their grief, little sparrow."

Skye *wailed*, the sound wrenched from the depths of her being.

She shrieked her loss and her gut-deep, burning anger, over and over, muffling the cries against warm flesh that did not quail or flinch away from the ugliness. Strong arms held her as the screams degenerated into weeping once more.

Her head felt like someone was driving a spike into it with every jerking sob. Her face was a river of snot and tears, and the disgusting, slimy mess formed an ever-expanding wet patch on the soft material of Hunter's shirt. Yet he merely continued to hold her until exhaustion finally overcame her, the sobs trailing off into small jerks, and finally, nothing.

She realized that she had somehow climbed half into his lap, and that his nose was buried in her hair. At any other moment in her life, she would have been horrified. She barely knew this man, this self-confessed criminal who was feared and hated by everyone in the Seven Systems with access to a news channel.

But she had also watched him strangle someone for threatening to touch her. She had watched him risk not just his life, but the lives of those he called friends to help her try to save the humans on Ilarius. She had eaten food directly from his hand; felt him tremble as her lips wrapped around his fingers.

There were the things people believed, and there was the truth. Skye had seen a glimpse of the truth hiding behind the shadow of The Rook. She had seen the truth of Hunter Tarthasian. And now he had seen the truth of her— or at least, most of it. And he hadn't turned away.

He should know the rest as well.

"My real mother died when I was small," she rasped, her voice scraped bare. "But my father remarried. She's trapped in a Regime cell somewhere. I don't know what they'll do to her now." She swallowed. "And I had a foster brother. Temple. He tried to act as a decoy when I stole the files, to keep me safe. I think… they may have killed him, too."

She pulled away, just enough to lift her red, watery eyes and meet his clear green ones. They seemed darker in the dimly lit sleeping room—a stormy sea at dusk.

"My entire family may have died to protect me," she continued. "It terrifies me that yours might die as well."

He regarded her for a long moment. She marveled once again at the contrast between the brutality of his scarred, tattooed features and the soulful depths of his eyes. How could any being have seen the things he must have seen—done the things he must have done—and still be able to show compassion?

"You are wrong," he said eventually. "Your family risked death to save the lives of many thousands, not just you. And we risk ourselves now for the same reason—to stop evil before it can destroy our world. Is that not a worthy reason to sacrifice oneself?"

Another hiccupping sob wracked her, but she swallowed it. "Yes." The word was a harsh whisper. "Of course it is."

The question was whether she would have enough courage to see it through, if it meant watching more people die.

ELEVEN

Hunter lifted a hand to wipe away the tear tracks marring Skye's face. She closed her eyes at his sure touch, leaning into it like a child. On some deep level where reason still ruled, he was appalled at the strength of his urge to protect her. To shelter her and make her his. How in the prophets' names had this *happened*?

Her tears were drying against his skin, stiffening the material of his shirt. He wanted to spirit her away to someplace safe—as if such a place existed for either of them now. He wanted to take her back into his arms. Draw her pain inside himself somehow, so the agony of fresh grief could no longer tear at her heart.

He wanted to kill, with his bare hands, every bastard that had ever hurt her or her family.

In short, he was forming a mating bond with her, and if he wasn't very, very careful, his horrendously bad timing was going to get all of them killed. But the worst part—the most painfully ridiculous part of the whole sorry mess—was that she didn't have the first clue what was happening.

Had she given herself over to his care because she felt some kind of a connection, too? Or because he was the only option for a few moments of safe haven when her burden finally became too heavy to bear? He didn't know, and it ate at him. But that was his problem, not hers.

Of course, Kade was going to burst a fucking aneurysm when he found out. He wasn't sure how the others would react. He *particularly* wasn't sure how Skye would react. It would probably be best not to even try to explain it to her. There was a very real possibility they'd all be dead soon anyway.

He took a slow, deep breath, attempting to ignore her human pheromones. They should have been so much nonsense to his Vithii senses, but they still managed, somehow, to convey the overwhelming message of *a female who needed him.*

He cleared his throat. "Ryder was right. You need to rest now."

She nodded, her eyes still closed, her cheek still pressed against the palm of his hand. "I'll try. Right now, my head feels like someone is pounding a steel spike into it, though."

He reluctantly broke contact, leaving her sitting on the edge of the bed, so he could retrieve a box of tissues sitting on a nearby table and bring it to her. She took it with a whispered word of thanks and blew her nose, avoiding eye contact with him. Embarrassed, perhaps, by her show of grief, though she had no reason to be.

"I'll see if there are any painkillers safe for humans to take," he told her. "Ryder will know."

She only nodded again, still not looking at him.

He dragged himself from her side and out of the room, cursing himself for ten kinds of fool as the door closed behind him.

Kade was waiting outside, returned from whatever backroom dealings he'd been engaged in to try to get them all the things they would need for this operation. He was leaning against the wall opposite the door with his arms crossed. Hunter stifled another sigh and walked up to him, stopping a step away. There was no point in putting off the inevitable.

Kade looked at the patch of wetness on the front of Hunter's shirt, then up at his face, then back at the wet patch. Hunter could see his nostrils flare, scenting the air. Cold gray eyes burned into his.

"You idiotic, suicidal fucker," Kade said in an absolutely flat tone, without moving or breaking pose. "What the ever-loving *fuck* are you *thinking*?"

Hunter felt his heightened instincts trying to rise to the open challenge from another male, and stifled them ruthlessly.

"It won't affect the mission," he said evenly.

"Of course it will affect the fucking mission." Kade pushed away from the wall and glared at him, obviously furious. "Give me one sane reason why I shouldn't take over leadership of this thing right now, before your *hormones* get us all killed."

Hunter swallowed the angry response that wanted to rise, knowing he owed Kade—and all of them—better than that. "One. You're too busy dealing with logistics to take over strategy and delegation as well. Two. Shaking things up now will alter the team dynamics in unforeseen ways and affect morale. Three. You're a neurotonin addict."

Kade held eye contact for a long time, as if searching for something.

Eventually, he spoke. "You'll discuss strategy with me before implementing it, and if I see you slipping, I'll step in before it becomes dangerous."

Hunter closed his eyes, unable to deny the relief he felt at having someone to keep him from making the kinds of mistakes that got people killed. Kade was not the right choice to lead this mission, but Hunter was undeniably in danger of being compromised—if he wasn't already. Between them, though… between them, maybe they could pull this off without it turning into a bloodbath.

"Agreed," he said, and clapped a hand on Kade's shoulder without opening his eyes, gripping hard. A moment later, a strong hand squeezed his forearm for an instant before dropping away. He heard Kade breathe in and out once, heavily.

Hunter let his hand slide away, and left for the lab without a backward glance.

The others were working, as he had expected they would be, but Ryder glanced up at his approach. "She all right? Do I need to come?"

Hunter shook his head. "Better now, I think. The Regime shot her father as she was escaping. He died right in front of her, and it was a messy death. Are there likely to be any painkillers here that are safe for humans?"

Ryder's face clouded at the explanation for Skye's noisy expression of grief, which had no doubt been audible throughout the compound. "Yeah, probably. Check the bathroom cabinets for acetaminophen. Don't let her have more than a thousand milligrams, no matter what the box says—their livers can't handle it."

"Right," he said.

The bathroom was reasonably well stocked, with a red and orange bottle of acetaminophen half-hidden at the back. He checked the dosage and shook out two white, oblong-shaped lozenges. When he re-entered the sleeping room with the pills and a cup of cool water, it was to find Skye sitting on top of the covers with her back against the wall, hugging her knees and staring at nothing.

"Take these," he said, "and sleep."

"I don't know if I can sleep right now," she said. Clogged sinuses lent her voice a congested, nasal quality. Her face was puffy. Her eyes, swollen and red.

He still couldn't look away from her.

"I'll stay until you do."

She glanced up at him, and back down at her knees. "The mission is more important than babysitting me."

He handed her the pills and the water. She took them without comment and swallowed them, tipping the water back until it was gone.

"No doubt you're right," he allowed. "But there is a reason I'm in here, and not out there wearing a white coat and goggles. The same reason you're not out there, in fact."

She met his eyes curiously. "No background in organic chemistry?"

"Or any other kind of chemistry," he said.

"But you're the leader here," she said. "Anyone can see that."

"And my role right now is to devise strategy," he replied, not denying it. "Which is somewhat difficult to do until Ash gets us information on the water treatment plant. So, for now, I can ponder hypothetical strategy here as effectively as I could in the lab—and I'll be less in the way. So, again—try to sleep, and I will stay here until you do."

She made no move to lie down, however.

"Tell me why you hate the Regime so much," she said instead.

The question should hardly have been a surprising one, and yet he was unprepared for it. *Behold, the master strategist at work*, he thought ruefully. *Blindsided by an exhausted human accountant. It's as well Kade isn't here to see this.*

"The Regime—or their supporters, rather—are responsible for the deaths of people dear to me," he said eventually. Hesitantly.

Hunter. Love you, sweetheart. Now run…

He blinked away the image of red, red human blood, creeping across concrete.

"Who?" Skye asked, the word a whisper.

"My… foster mothers," he said. He was reluctant to speak of it, but perhaps she deserved to know something of the similarities between them.

She frowned. "Mothers? Wait, you mean, like, lesbians? But I thought Vithii didn't have homosexual relationships—"

"That's the official line, certainly," he said. "However, they were not Vithii. My biological parents were killed in a hovercar crash when I was eleven. The Party considered them radicals. They shunned us. There was no help for me from official channels when I was orphaned. I ended up on the streets."

Skye looked appalled. "At eleven years old? How did you survive?"

"The way all street children survive. Any way I could." His eyes grew unfocused at the memory. "One afternoon, I tried to steal from an apartment owned by a human couple. I was sure when I broke in that they were gone—they were always gone at that time of day. But they weren't. They were inside. They took one look at me, sat me down, and fed me the first decent meal I'd had in weeks. Before I knew it, I was spending more time there than I was hustling on the street. They adopted me in all but name. Looked after me. Tried… to keep me safe."

"What happened?" she asked softly.

Red, red human blood, forming an ever-expanding puddle on the pavement beneath him.

"Some members of the Vithii First movement got wind of what was happening. They might not have given two fucks about me when I was starving on the street, but they weren't about to stand for a Vithii kid being raised by two human women who loved each other."

He could hear the bitterness creeping into his tone, but he continued.

"Our apartment was on the fifth floor of the complex. I was out looking for odd jobs when a mob barricaded the doors to the flat and set fire to it, with Muriel and Alex trapped inside. I saw the smoke as I was walking home. When I realized it was coming from our building, I started running. I arrived just as the two of them jumped out of the window to escape the flames, clasped in each others' arms as they fell."

Skye gasped, her hand flying to her mouth.

He continued in a monotone. "They were both horribly burned. When I reached them, Muriel's neck was broken, but Alex was still alive. She begged me to run before the mob caught me. I—" The word caught in his throat for a moment. "—did."

He looked up to find that Skye was crying again.

Crying. For him. For two women she had never met.

"Bastards," she whispered hoarsely. "Fucking *bastards*. I swear I won't rest until they pay for the things they've done."

Before he realized what was happening, she was in his arms again, embracing him fiercely as if trying to comfort him for an injury that had closed up and scarred over years ago, the flesh left behind ugly and twisted.

"We will make them pay," he assured her, no more able to stop his own arms from closing around her than he could stop the sun from rising or the tide from turning. "We have dedicated our lives to making them pay, sparrow. But first we must stop them from committing even more senseless murder."

She nodded against his chest. "Yes."

He could feel her trembling. She was exhausted. Tears still squeezed from behind her closed eyelids. Perhaps it was good that someone was finally grieving his lost guardians, as they deserved to be grieved. He had never mourned them in the Vithii way. Revenge came first, he'd always told himself. Grieving would have to wait until the Regime had paid the price for their cruelty.

And if death claimed Hunter before that debt was paid? Well, perhaps if there was justice in the universe, he would see them again in the afterlife, and be able to thank them for the gift they'd given him as a boy.

It was a nice dream, anyway.

He eased down onto the edge of the bed, urging Skye around until she was pressed against his side while he sat with his back leaning against the headboard, her head pillowed against his shoulder. She continued to cling to him, even as her mind finally gave up the fight against sleep. He felt her muscles relax, her body sinking into his as her congested breathing evened out.

The effect she had on him was terrifying, yet he could not find it in himself to wish that he'd never met her. If a platoon of Regime soldiers burst into the lab tomorrow and shot him dead, he would die a happy man with the memory of this fragile human sleeping in his arms, showing him such complete trust.

He closed his eyes, his brow furrowing.

He had to keep control. There was too much at stake. This wasn't about him. It wasn't even about her. This was about genocide in the city they both called home.

It was about the future. He couldn't afford to make mistakes. No matter what.

TWELVE

When Skye woke much later, she was alone. Her head still pounded with a dull, throbbing ache. Her eyes felt like sandpaper, and her stomach muscles hurt from sobbing.

Her heart was still heavy with grief.

But she no longer felt as though she were losing her mind. She was… *present*. She was *here*, in this borrowed bed where some underpaid mob drone usually slept after a day of manufacturing illegal drugs. She was *here*, in a rented lab surrounded by the members of a Vithii criminal gang reviled throughout the sector.

Including the man who had held her as she wept, and told her about the time he saw his only family die horribly at the hands of a Firster mob, when he was only a child.

No wonder he hated the members of his own species who would see the humans on Ilarius dead or enslaved. She wondered what kinds of stories lived in the others' pasts. What had turned Ryder against her own people? What had turned Kade? Or Pax, or Draven? She knew better than to ask. She was still surprised, quite frankly, that she'd been brave enough to ask Hunter—and even more surprised that he'd answered.

She might have been mired in her own emotional loss, but she knew she had to move forward anyway. "Shower," she decided, forcing stiff muscles and joints into motion. There was a chrono on the wall next to the door. It was late in the morning, and she felt a flush of embarrassment at the idea of having slept in like some kind of spoiled college undergrad on her day off, given what was at stake.

It was too late to do anything about it now, though, so she contented herself with padding to the bathroom and scoping out the towel situation. The water was blissfully hot and came out of the showerhead with more pressure than it ever had back home in her crappy little apartment. She let it pour over her, washing away days of sweat and grime. The soap was unscented, harsh and industrial. She couldn't find anything that looked like shampoo, so she reluctantly used the soap on her hair and scalp, as well.

The towel was threadbare, and a bit scratchy as she scrubbed it over her pink skin. In the absence of a comb, she ran her fingers through squeaky tangles of hair and fashioned it into a messy French braid while it was still damp, tucking the end of the plait under to—hopefully—keep it from coming loose for a while.

She eyed her torn and stained jumpsuit with distaste. Maybe this would be a good time to go looking for one of those oversized Vithii lab coats. Though that wouldn't do anything to help with the single pair of dirty underpants which were all she now possessed, or the socks that she'd been wearing for days.

On the one hand, she knew that worrying about things like clean underwear when a bioweapon was about to be released into the city was ridiculous. And yet, perhaps worrying about such small things was her brain's way of coping with everything else that was happening around her. She sighed and wrapped a towel around her body, gathering up her dirty clothes and peeking up and down the hallway to make sure the coast was clear before hurrying back to her borrowed bedroom.

A crisp new, black flightsuit was waiting on the bed, along with an unmarked bag containing simple white polysynth underwear. She stared at it for a long moment. The sweat-stained *seelaht* costume fell from numb fingers to the scuffed gray carpet, and she practically lunged at the clean, fresh clothing.

It was a testament to how far out of it she still was that it didn't occur to her to question where it had come from until after she was already dressed and staring at herself in the small wall mirror. The woman staring back at her was red-eyed and pale, but at least she looked marginally human again.

"I still don't forgive you for what you did, Daddy," she told the empty room, "but I'm trying my best to make it right. They haven't beaten us yet. Not *yet*. We're still fighting."

There was a buzz at the door.

"Yes?" she called.

It opened, revealing Hunter. Skye felt heat rise to her cheeks as she remembered just how many barriers she'd let fall between them. What must he think of her? But he merely frowned and looked around the small room.

"Who were you talking to?" he asked.

After everything he'd seen last night, there was no point in trying to lie.

"Only the dead," she told him. "They say that talking to yourself is the first sign of madness. I'm not sure where talking to ghosts falls on the list."

His expression smoothed out. "As long as they don't start talking back, I wouldn't worry too much."

That surprised a snort from her. It was the first thing approximating a joke she'd ever heard from him. "I'll keep that in mind," she said. She looked down at the clothing she was wearing, and back up at him. "Where did this flightsuit come from, anyway? I need to thank whoever's responsible. It even fits pretty well."

He waved it off. "It's nothing, don't worry about it."

"It's not nothing," she said. "But, well—if I can't thank you for the clothes, then at least tell me what I've missed while I've been asleep."

"Ash contacted Kade with preliminary information about the water treatment plant. We have a set of building plans for the place now, though they're several years old. Kade, Pax, and I have been discussing our options for getting inside."

Skye's heart beat faster. "So, you think it can be done?"

He shrugged. "It's not precisely a soft target, but it's not a hard target either. Getting in might not be too difficult, though getting in with a tank full of antidote and a bunch of nanotech will be something of an added challenge. As I said, we've been discussing our options. You should join us before Kade has to leave again, so you can get an idea of what we're looking at."

She nodded, already heading for the door. "Right. What about the antidote itself? How's it coming along?"

He paced her, slowing his long strides to match hers so she didn't have to jog to keep up. "Draven and Ryder assure me it's progressing as well as can be expected. Apparently it's not the sort of thing that can be hurried."

A frown slid over her face, but she smoothed it away consciously. "Just so His Fucking Eminence the Bastard-In-Chief doesn't decide to start spraying bio-agents into the air before it's done."

"We can only control the things we can control, sparrow," Hunter said. "The rest is a waste of energy and resources. What you said, though—do you know more details about the weapon? What form it will take? I should have asked earlier."

His face darkened, as if he was irritated with himself for the oversight.

"It's an aerosol containing particles of the bio-agent," she explained. "That's all I know."

"Then an atmospheric release from aircraft seems the likeliest delivery system," said Hunter. "If it were in hostile territory, cluster bombs would make more sense, but that's hardly practical in the Capital. At any rate, like the antidote, such things cannot be produced overnight. Though, of course, we have no way of knowing how far along they are in the process."

They arrived at the little kitchen-slash-cantina, where Pax and Kade were seated at a long folding table. Both of them looked up at her entrance. Pax's expression was neutral as always, but Skye thought she detected hostility behind Kade's cold gaze.

"Um… hi," she said, unable to keep the hesitance from her tone or the blood from staining her cheeks at the realization that both of these frightening, powerful men had probably heard her wailing and weeping like an injured child the previous evening. She swallowed. "Sorry… uh… sorry for all the ruckus last night. I didn't mean to be a distraction. Everything just kind of... hit me at once, I guess..."

And, indeed, her grief randomly chose that moment to surge up again, burning at the backs of her eyes and trying to block her throat. But she was *not* going there right now. Not in front of Kade, who had raised an eyebrow and looked meaningfully at Hunter when she'd said *I didn't mean to be a distraction*. Not in front of a cyborg who'd had his emotion centers ripped out by the Regime's military researchers. Not in front of Hunter, who had already been exposed to more of her shit in the space of a single day than any sane man would voluntarily sign up for.

She shoved everything down and away, searching for the numbness that had served her well up until this point.

Oddly, it was Pax who answered. "The biological mind always grieves its losses. There is no shame in it."

There was no detectable sympathy or feeling of any kind behind the flat words, but she still said, "Thanks." The word emerged hoarsely, and she cleared her throat. "Hunter says you've got plans to the water treatment plant?"

Pax nodded. "Ash will be meeting with his Regime contact again tomorrow night, and may have additional information to offer at that time. Until then, we can at least discuss options for infiltration into the site."

Kade seemed to shake himself free of whatever resentment he harbored against her and returned to the matter at hand. He shoved a sleek data padd toward the center of the table and thumbed the power button. A 3-D holographic representation of a large complex of buildings and tanks flickered into life above the screen.

"The current water system was constructed not long after the Vithii refugees first arrived on Ilarius," Kade said. "It was built during peacetime, with very little thought given to security beyond the basics that you'd find in any example of public infrastructure. Some attempt has been made in recent years to tighten it up, but there's only so much you can do to a facility that has people and shipments of chemicals coming in almost every day."

Skye latched onto his words, her earlier awkwardness falling away. "Wait. *Shipments of chemicals*, you said?"

"She's quick off the mark," Pax observed.

Hunter nodded. "It's a water *treatment* plant. And they treat the water with things that have to be shipped in. Chlorine. Polyelectrolytes. Even fresh deliveries of carbon filtration media."

She was getting properly excited now. "But, that's our way in! We just need to pose as one of those delivery crews, with a tank full of nanobots and antidote instead of chlorine, then pipe it straight into the system!"

Kade eyed her with a jaundiced expression. "*Just*, she says. Tell you what—you get right on that, why don't you? Let us know when you're ready."

"*Kade*," Hunter said, warning in his tone.

She didn't back down, even though the gray-eyed Vithii's open hostility made her heart beat faster. "Is it or is it not a more realistic plan than charging in with blasters firing and trying to take the place by force?"

"Of course it is," said Pax. "Which isn't to say it's without complications."

Kade snorted in obvious disgust. "If by *not without complications*, you mean *like something out of a bad holodrama that's likely to end in disaster*, then, yeah."

"It's a place to start," Hunter said firmly. "We need to find out if the delivery crews can be bribed, and if not, what the most vulnerable point is where we could take one of the tankers, ideally without attracting immediate attention. Also, what sort of uniforms the crews wear, how many accompany each tanker, and whether it would be better to transport the antidote to the tanker or bring the tanker here to pick up the antidote from the lab. How does Jago normally get his drugs out of the lab?"

"Ask Draven," Kade said, still sour. "He'll know the basics."

"Right." Hunter looked from one to the other of them. "Pax, tell Draven he's due for a break, and talk to him about the best way to get materials from the lab to a stolen tanker truck. Kade, try to get us a contact at one of the treatment plant's suppliers. I'm guessing the polyelectrolyte transfer vehicles would be better suited for our use than the ones designed for chlorine gas?"

"Almost certainly," Pax confirmed.

Kade drummed his fingers on the cheap plastic table. "There's some experimental tech I want to get my hands on before we try to pull this off. It's expensive. Also, illegal to possess—outside of a research setting, anyway. I may have to start selling off assets to pay for it."

Hunter shrugged. "Get whatever you need, however you have to. You don't need my permission for that shit, Kade. You never have."

Mollified, Kade nodded and got to his feet. "I'll be in touch. Don't worry if you don't hear from me for a day or so."

Hunter gave him a sharp look. "You'll have enough injections with you for that long on your own?"

Kade stiffened. "Believe it or not, *tei'laal*, I have managed to deal with my *little problem* successfully on my own for a very long time, now."

THIRTEEN

Kade left without another word, though not without throwing Skye a brief, dark glance as he swept through the door. She felt Hunter's sigh, more than she heard it. Pax rose, his flat gaze falling on first her, then Hunter.

"I'll talk to Draven and keep you posted on what we decide," said the cyborg.

"Make sure Ryder takes a break, while you're at it," Hunter replied. "She's pushing a full day without sleep already."

A moment later, the two of them were alone in the little break room. The prospect of more time with nothing to do except think stretched out in front of Skye. Even with the first sharp edges of her grief worn away, the idea was daunting.

"Is there anything I can do?" she asked. "Anything at all?"

Hunter looked down at her, his green eyes not without compassion. "There may be some busy work in the lab, though most of it seems to be automated. And you can monitor the private comms for messages on Ash's frequency while the others rest. Mostly, though, it will be a waiting game for both of us."

She nodded. "What about you? What will you be doing?"

"Thinking," he said. "Thinking… and waiting. It's safer for me not to go out unless it's really necessary. I'm too recognizable, and the last thing we need is unwanted attention. Until the real action starts, I'm a liability."

For some reason, the idea that she wasn't the only one relegated to sitting around while the others worked made her feel a little better. Still, it was obvious that Hunter had a role to play here that she, as an outsider with no scientific credentials, did not. The effortless way he had taken control and subtly directed the others was in no way lost on her.

Without him, Kade, Pax, and the rest would have been a group of random criminals and fugitives. It was his presence that molded them into a cohesive whole. In some ways, she got the impression that he *was* the Shadow Wing. She remembered something Kade had said to her, shortly after she'd discovered that they were all on more or less the same side.

"As soon as you said 'fight the Regime,' I imagine you had Hunter on board. And if he's on board, then the rest of us will inevitably be dragged along for the ride."

This was Hunter's war they were fighting. Not that the others weren't willing soldiers in that war… they were. Nothing about their behavior indicated that they had been coerced into doing this. Quite the opposite. They were passionate about ending the Regime. But Skye was willing to bet that without Hunter, they would not be here with her now, taking steps to enact a crazy plan and execute a nearly impossible countermove against the Premiere.

She was frankly terrified to lose more people— people for whom she was already beginning to care. To care *deeply*, in one case. But her life had not been her own since Temple had told her what their father had done. Her life belonged to the human population of the Capital now. And she supposed the others' lives did too, since they'd decided to act with her.

It was *their* war now, and she would do whatever it took to show Hunter that she was in it with them. She only wished there was more for her to *actually do*. Hunter had called himself a liability. But she knew that *she* was the true liability here.

———◆———

The day dragged. That night, alone in her borrowed room, she barely slept. The following day was even worse. Not because of any real problems—as far as she could tell, everything was going as smoothly as it could under the circumstances. Kade had returned safely around midday, and Ryder reported that the latest generation of bots was in the process of synthesizing a small test batch of the antidote.

Everything was fine. Everything except Skye. By late afternoon, she had given up trying to hold back the tears of grief that kept trying to burn their way out from behind her eyes. It was a different sort of grieving than the rage-filled shrieks of denial she'd muffled against Hunter's broad chest. This was the sudden grief of realizing that she would never hug her father again. Or laugh with Temple over some stupid holodrama. Or see the inside of her pathetic little work cubicle at the university's administration building.

So she sat by the comm unit that Ash would use to contact them when he had news, and let the tears slide down her face unchecked. She ate when Hunter brought her food and set it down in front of her, crossing his arms until she finished and shoved the empty packaging away.

He seemed... distant, somehow, which was probably a ridiculous thing for her to even think. His silent regard should not seem unusual or unexpected. If anything, their brief connection on the night she had broken down was the oddity, not this.

And yet—

Well. It was hardly like she could say anything about it to him. What would she even say?

So, she sat at the comm panel and cried intermittently. She ate the food he brought her and drank the tea and tried not to go nuts from thinking too much. And the day dragged on. Finally, Pax came into the little room and told her to go rest, that he would monitor Ash's frequency for the next few cycles.

Maybe tonight she'd be tired enough to just *sleep*. She thought longingly of the way she'd drifted off in Hunter's arms two nights ago—pounding head, clogged nose and all. Then she berated herself for thinking it. What was she going to do, walk up to him and ask him to tuck her in?

Prophets, she was *pathetic*.

She thanked Pax and dragged her pitiful ass back to wash up, unbraid her hair, and pull off her boots. She'd been sleeping clothed—okay, she'd been lying on her bed staring at the ceiling in the darkness clothed—because it made her feel just slightly better prepared on the off chance that Regime soldiers burst into the lab in the middle of the night to arrest them all.

So she closed the door behind her, checked the alarm function on the chrono, and pulled back the thin coverlet on the bed before flopping down on it. "Lights off," she said, and threw a forearm across her eyes as the overhead lighting dimmed obligingly.

Gods, she really was exhausted. Maybe she'd be able to sleep after all. If only she could do it without dreaming…

✦

It was late, but Hunter still sat slouched in the molded duraplast chair next to the small writing desk in the quarters he'd claimed as his own, thinking. Running over and over the same set of possibilities, trying to get the best angle, the best approach. The chair was tipped back on two legs, and one booted foot rested on the edge of the desk, which had, for some obscure reason, been bolted to the floor.

He had been, he thought, fairly successful in not letting his thrice-damned hormones call the shots over the course of the last day-and-a-half. Kade would be proud of him.

All right. That was a lie.

Kade would tell him to fuck off, because he was busy trying to make impossible deals on an impossible schedule in pursuit of an impossible mission objective. But, anyway. Things were, for the moment, more or less under control. The only immediate worry was Ash, who at this moment was no doubt entering the lion's den, bartering his own safety for the possibility of gaining sensitive information from a government lackey with sick tastes and an overblown opinion of his own importance.

Those are the best kind, Ash would say. *They love to brag in the afterglow about all the important things they're privy to.*

The thought of it made Hunter vaguely queasy. But then, it always did. Ash made his own decisions. If he ever got in over his head, the rest of them would tear the Capital apart to try and pull him out. For now, though, he seemed content to continue on his reckless path—and Hunter could not deny that without the information Ash gleaned from his unwitting marks, they would never have been able to act in time to stop the Premiere's latest insane plan.

A faint noise penetrated his musing. Hunter let the chair fall back onto four legs, listening intently. A frown creased his forehead as it came again. It wasn't the sort of sound he could picture coming from any of the other Vithii in the lab compound, and that meant—

He was on his feet before he knew it, striding through the open door of his room and into the hallway beyond. There it was again—a gasping sob, quickly stifled. He didn't even think before palming the sensor on Skye's door—instinct propelled him to her side without it even occurring to him that he should knock, or call her name first. By the time civilized thought caught up, it was too late.

He was already in her room, his eyes adjusting quickly to the dim glow from the chrono's glowing red numbers. She was sitting up.

"*Lights*," she croaked, and the room's illumination flared into life.

She was fully dressed, her legs tangled in the old military surplus blanket that covered the bed.

Her breath was coming in gasps, but she did not seem alarmed by his sudden intrusion.

Instead, she looked up at him, disheveled and unguarded. She was already forcing her ragged breathing under control.

"I had a dream," she said. "Except it's probably real."

"What did you dream?" he asked, still standing frozen inside her doorway.

"My fish," she said. "They're dead."

He looked at her, and his confusion must have been obvious, because she continued, "I keep an aquarium of fish in my apartment, as pets. I was so upset after Temple contacted me and told me what our father had done, I didn't even think about giving them away or getting someone to look after them before I left to try and help him smuggle the data crystal out." She swallowed. "They're native Ilarian saltwater bluespinners. The little delicate kind. They will have died by now, without care."

Hunter didn't claim to be an expert on human emotions surrounding fish ownership, but somehow the oversight didn't quite seem like something that would rise to the level of nightmare fodder.

"You had other things to worry about," he said.

She shook her head. "No, you don't understand. My father entrusted the lives of tens of thousands of people to me, and *I can't even keep a tank of fish alive.*"

He took a step toward her without intending to. The door slid shut automatically behind him. "Yet, you are here. Outside that door, nanobots are synthesizing the formula you brought us, and Kade is arranging for its transport. We may yet save those thousands. And… I ate fish only a handful of days ago. It was, as I recall, quite good."

If he'd hoped to somehow lighten the atmosphere with the pitiful attempt at humor, he had failed. She looked up at him with wide blue eyes, as if trying to see straight through skin and bone to what lay hidden beneath.

"I can't bear this unending feeling of hopelessness and loss, Hunter," she said. "For days now, I've swung back and forth between feeling like I'm dead inside to feeling like my heart is going to shatter into pieces. Like it's being stabbed with a knife."

"Sparrow…" he began, but she shook her head.

"The only time I've been at peace was when you were holding me in your arms," she said, still not breaking his gaze. "You've felt the connection between us, too. I *know* you have, even if you've been trying to keep your distance."

His hands twitched with the need to reach out to her, but he kept them at his sides with iron will. "Getting too close to me would be unwise, Skye. I'm not a safe individual to be around."

"And you think I am?" A crease formed on her forehead. Hunter could not look away from the small mark of discontent. "There's a very real chance that we're going to die soon, or be captured—which is probably even worse. I *can't* feel like this any more. I need to feel… something else. Something better. Even if it's only for a night. Please, Hunter. *Please…*"

There could be no question of what she was asking for, and the realization hit him in the chest like a roundhouse kick from Pax. Buried need reared up, so powerful and instinctual that it frightened him.

A female who needed him.

"Little sparrow," he asked, barely recognizing his own voice. His mouth was dry. "Are you... begging me?"

FOURTEEN

Skye looked up at him, perplexed, but then a half-forgotten memory percolated through her confusion. She'd been in the medbay on the lunar base. Ash had just discovered the data crystal hidden in her earring, and had called Hunter. She was convinced that they would torture her, and was imagining all sorts of horrors.

When Hunter ordered the others from the room, she immediately assumed that sexual assault would be the first item on the menu, ludicrous though the idea seemed now, looking back.

"You're going to rape me," she'd said.

A look of cold scorn had crossed his coarse features, and his tone was one of utter contempt. "I prefer my sex partners to be begging before I take them, little sparrow."

Of course, at the time, she'd taken it as a threat. Now, though...

Now, she understood.

She'd thought her strange attraction to him to be one-sided, but it wasn't. He had saved her, when letting her die would have been far safer for him. Aided her, when she had no one else to turn to. Protected her. Trembled at the touch of her lips against his fingertips. Held her as she'd grieved. Shared a part of his wounded heart with her. Trusted her with a piece of his painful past.

And now, here he was in her room in the middle of the night, staring at her like he wanted to wrap her in his arms and never let her go, because he'd heard her cry out during a nightmare.

But even now, she could tell that he still needed to be sure. His hands were curling into fists, practically vibrating with the battle to stay still until he had her answer. He was overpoweringly male, in the way that only Vithii could be. Heavy brow, square chin, rippling muscles… and depthless green eyes that formed a window straight to the huge, compassionate heart that beat inside that solid chest.

"Touch me, Hunter," she said, very deliberately. "Please. I need you tonight. I'm begging you."

She wasn't sure what to expect, and honestly, right now she didn't care. What she got was a low growl that rumbled up from the depths of his chest, an instant before he was looming over her, one hand braced next to her on the mattress, and the other cradling her cheek, sliding down the side of her neck, and tangling in the unzipped collar of the clothing he'd somehow acquired for her.

His strong grip could easily have torn the rugged synthetic material like tissue, and she shivered.

"Off," he said. "Get this *off*, or you'll have two ripped jumpsuits instead of just one."

She scrabbled for the closures, fumbling as he used his grip to yank the material aside and fasten lips and teeth on the column of her neck. She gasped, bright pinpricks of sensation shivering their way down her spine as he nipped along the taut line of tendon.

Finally, the stays holding the triangular flap across her chest slipped free, exposing the zip underneath. Hunter grasped the pull-tab and slid it down. There was something of an air of finality to the rasp of metallic teeth as the jumpsuit parted, revealing her body to his gaze.

He pulled back, but only enough to let her struggle out of the top half of the one-piece outfit, leaving her bare above the waist except for her practical white brassiere. When her arms were free, she reached for him, not about to wait another minute to see what lay beneath the dark, form-fitting shirt he wore. Hunter allowed her to tug it free of his waistband, before he grasped the hem in both hands and pulled it over his head in one smooth movement.

The tattoos stretched over his chest and stomach, graceful swirls of black feathers marred here and there by old scars that told the tale of a lifelong struggle for survival. His muscles flexed under her hand as she ran a palm from his sternum to his navel, then lower, reaching for the fastening of his fly.

Powerful fingers closed around her wrist, fast as a striking snake. Her bones felt like the delicate bones of a bird under his sure grip.

"If we start this now, I may not be able to stop," he told her.

She looked up, meeting his earnest green gaze. Maybe she should have been scared, she thought, remembering schoolgirl whispers about Vithii men and what they could do. But all the fright had been burned out of her over the past few days. Sex between the two species might have been taboo, but Vithii and humans obviously *could* mate, or else *seelahts* would not exist. Right now, that was all she needed to know.

"You're doing better than me, in that case," she told him, never breaking eye contact. "I already can't stop."

Hunter breathed out as if he'd been punched—a sharp exhalation. The grip on her wrist guided her hand back to his trousers and pressed it over the bulge there. She cupped his length, already hard and twitching for her, feeling an answering surge of wetness between her own legs.

He let her go, only to drag the tangled blanket free from her legs, where she'd kicked it during her dream. Then he grasped the material of the jumpsuit around her waist and pulled it down, his fingers hooking into the band of her underwear at the same time.

The touch of his skin against hers was like a brand. She shimmied out of the clothing, lifting her hips to help him get it off. The white brassiere had a front clasp, thankfully, and she made short work of it even with her unsteady fingers. A moment later, she was completely bare under his hot gaze.

"You, too," she insisted, looking up at him as he loomed over her. "Let me see. I want to see…"

He didn't linger in removing the rest of his clothing, toeing off his heavy boots and stepping out of his trousers. She stared unabashedly—he was chiseled and beautifully proportioned. His cock, while larger than any of the human men she'd slept with over the years, was not unnaturally huge.

There's one schoolgirl rumor out the window, she thought. Which—okay—was actually quite a relief. It had been almost a year since she'd broken up with her last partner. To say she was out of practice was putting it mildly.

"Can I look?" she asked breathlessly, curiosity momentarily overcoming lust as she knelt on the edge of the bed to look at him.

His hand smoothed over her temple, tangling in her long hair and rubbing the strands together between his fingers.

"Not so different, is it?" he asked, his voice low and rough.

Feeling bold, she wrapped him in a loose fist and slid her hand up and down, once, drawing a groan from him. There *were* differences, though, and they intrigued her.

He had no obvious scrotum, though there was a slight bulge behind the base of his erection that might have been analogous. There was also a ridge of tissue around the circumference of his shaft, roughly halfway up the length. The texture of it was different, and she felt him tremble as her hand rubbed over it. Perhaps most striking, though, was the way the tip quivered and moved as she fisted him, probing from side to side as if seeking something.

A flush of heat ran through her at the thought of it inside her—moving, exploring, feeling its way around.

"No. Not so different," she agreed, her voice throaty. She sat back so she could look at him properly. "Gods, Hunter... you look like some ancient carving of a Greek hero."

"And you look like the marble statues that artists used to make of mythical forest sprites. So graceful and delicate."

She blushed, ridiculous though it might have been. No one had ever called her *graceful* in her life. She was the clumsy one. The one that was too tall and gawky, always stumbling over her own feet. But… the way Hunter was looking at her now, like she was a feast spread out before him—

She could almost believe his words. For this moment in time, at least.

An unwelcome thought intruded, but it would have been foolish not to ask. "Wait… do we, uh, need protection? Is there anything here we can use? Not for pregnancy, obviously—" She was well aware that Vithii-human hybrids couldn't happen spontaneously. But that wasn't the only concern with unprotected sex.

"I'm reliably informed that our species are too different to share any diseases," Hunter said. "Besides which, I haven't been exposed to anything in recent memory. I have not bedded a woman in a very long time."

It was well known that humans and Vithii couldn't pass common contagious diseases to each other, so what he said made sense. The second part surprised her, though.

It must have shown on her face, because he said, "My current circumstances aren't what you'd call *conducive*, I'm afraid," with a faint, wry twist of the lips.

She huffed a breath. "Yeah, I guess not. Well, if it makes you feel better, I'm coming off a dry spell myself, and with far less justification."

"Then the men in your life were fools," he said. "Now, if you've looked your fill, sparrow, it's my turn."

He didn't wait for an answer, stalking forward onto the bed as she scuttled back to make room for him. She ended up on her back underneath him, caged by his powerful arms and legs, her heart pounding in anticipation as he gazed down at her.

"Not so different?" she asked, barely a whisper.

"That remains to be seen," he said, and lowered himself to once again nip his way down her throat. This time, he continued lower, exploring her breasts with his teeth and tongue. She bit her lip and arched up, offering herself to him, desperate for this feeling of pleasure and wanting after so long spent mired in grief and despair.

She cried out softly when his sharp teeth closed around a nipple, his tongue flicking at the pebbled tip. When she was panting with need, he abandoned her breasts in favor of nibbling his way down her stomach. She grabbed the bed frame with both hands to keep from grabbing him instead, knowing that he also needed a chance to explore her body and map out her differences.

The lights were still shining at full strength, and she felt deliciously exposed as he lifted her right leg to the side. A large, callused hand cupped her sex. His fingertips slid along the crease of her labia, slippery from her growing excitement.

"So wet," he breathed.

Hunter parted her folds and explored inside. She was already wound up to the point that the tentative touch felt like a live wire against her skin. A finger delved inside her, and she arched her hips into the contact, clenching around it. A second finger slid farther back, playing over the pucker of her ass. She hissed, and rocked against him again.

"No—you are not so different, either." From the tone of the words, she thought that he must be smiling. "But, where is your—?"

His thumb slid forward, dragging over her clit unexpectedly. She cried out and writhed against the mattress.

"Ah," he said. "A bit different after all, I see—but I think I can work with that."

With no further warning, he bent his head and licked a stripe up her inner labia to her clit, his thick finger still buried in her passage.

"Oh, gods—" Skye felt her eyes roll back, and gripped the bed frame until her knuckles turned white. "Yes… yes, like that… don't stop…"

Hunter obviously had no intention of stopping. He explored her with fingers and tongue, never letting up until she went rigid, and jerked through a powerful release that left her lightheaded and dazed. She was only half aware of him crawling back up the length of her body; settling himself in the cradle of her thighs.

The brush of his thumb over her lower lip brought her back to herself. He pressed it into her willing mouth, and fresh desire slammed into her as she remembered the first moment when she'd realized she was affecting him, as he'd fed her bites of food at Jago's table.

She stretched up, taking him deep—laving and sucking as her oversensitive sex twitched and pulsed, begging to be filled in the same way. He made that wonderful rumbling noise in his chest again, and slid his thumb free of her mouth with a soft pop.

"Wicked little minx," he growled, and thrust his hips against hers.

"You love it," she accused. His hard cock slid between her labia, the strange ridge rubbing across oversensitive nerves and making her voice go wobbly on the last word.

Rather than answer in words, he smiled down at her, changed the angle of his hips, and slid inside her with a slow thrust.

FIFTEEN

The feeling was so perfect that she let her head fall back, baring her throat and panting for air. He might not have been unnaturally huge, but he was still generously endowed. The burn as her body stretched to accommodate him was *exactly* what she needed, and the feeling as the stretch transformed into deep, throbbing pleasure was divine.

Gods, if they could just do this all night, she would be able to forget *everything*. He settled onto his elbows, his large frame pressing hers into the soft mattress, but not crushing her. He pulled almost all of the way out and slid in, as she arched up to meet him.

"So good," he murmured, the words tickling the shell of her ear. "You feel so good around me. Let me keep you here like this tonight, little sparrow. Let me take care of you."

She nodded, ridiculous tears burning behind her eyes. She needed what he was offering so badly it ached. "Yes, please," she whispered. "Please, Hunter… just like this."

He lifted a hand to stroke a strand of sweat-dampened hair back from her forehead, and she closed her eyes, savoring the feeling. Taking more of his weight on his muscular arms, he established a purposeful rhythm, pumping into her with measured, powerful strokes.

She had barely settled into the tempo when he tensed above her and pulsed into her with a series of warm spurts, filling her with his seed.

Oh, she thought. *Well, damn.*

It was difficult to swallow her disappointment, as all her hopes of a night of pleasure-drugged oblivion came abruptly crashing back to the ground.

Stupid, Skye. You're being stupid. He told you right up front that it had been a long time for him. That's what you get for building up ridiculous expectations on the strength of schoolyard rumors about Vithii males and sex. Besides, you've got no reason to complain—he gave you one hell of an orgasm already. And maybe he'll want to go again later. He might have more stamina the second time.

She wriggled a bit, preparing to help him disengage, but he pressed her down with his body, keeping her in place.

"Shh," he said, a depth of calm serenity entering his voice that she had not heard in him before. "Stay still for a moment, beloved. Not long now."

He was still inside her. Still hard. And… something new was happening. The wonderful, deep stretch from earlier had returned, as if he was somehow *growing* inside of her. An overwhelming feeling of fullness made her gasp, her eyes flying to his in confusion.

"What—?" she said. "*Ah!* What's happening?"

Hunter's pale green eyes had grown dark, the pupils blown wide. Again, he stroked gentle fingers over her hair, that same calm, reassuring timbre to his voice as he replied, "I'm knotting you. Be still—let it happen, and then we will rest here together. All is well."

"Oh, my *gods*," Skye managed. The knot was pressing against the sensitive place on the front wall of her passage that had always made her melt whenever a man was lucky enough to find it. A moment later, something brushed across her cervix—the prehensile tip of his cock that she'd marveled at earlier, probing at the entrance to her womb.

Her arms and legs began to quiver. The implications settled over her slowly—he meant them to stay like this, while his magic alien cock held her in place with its swollen knot and rubbed against all of her most sensitive places, never stopping or letting up—

She moaned, and a rolling, full-body orgasm washed over her like a wave, dragging her under. Hunter held her, steadying her until she surfaced with a gasp.

"Skye?" he asked, a hint of worry creeping into his tone. "Easy, now. Are you all right? Try to relax…"

She stared up at him, her mouth open. "Try to *relax*? Are you *joking*?"

Her passage was fluttering around his swollen knot, sending new shocks of pleasure through her even as the tip of his cock tried to wriggle and tease its way even deeper inside her, waking nerves that had never been touched in such a way before. Already, she was building toward another climax, her skin going hot, then cold, then hot again.

But she could tell Hunter was growing alarmed.

"Am I hurting you?" he asked. "Separating from a Vithii female during knotting can cause injury, but you don't seem to have a vaginal sphincter, so maybe if I was careful, I could try pulling out—"

"*Don't you fucking dare*," she said quickly, wrapping her legs around him to keep him from even *thinking* about it. "Prophets—you're not hurting me! Quite the—" She gasped as he rubbed against her walls in just *exactly* the right way. "*Ah!* Quite the opposite…"

He relaxed above her, understanding dawning in his expression. "*Oh.* I… uh, didn't realize it would have that effect on you. You're all right, then?"

A sharp bark of laughter escaped her throat, the little jolt sending yet another surge along over-stimulated nerves. "All right? I am *fucking phenomenal.* You can't possibly be trying to tell me that Vithii women don't come from this?"

"Once, usually, while the male is rutting," he said, still watching her closely. "After that, they slip into a coital trance for the duration of the knotting. I'm told it's very peaceful for them. I apologize for the lack of warning—I didn't know humans were so different in that respect."

Another laugh tried to bubble up. "*Don't* apologize. Just tell me, will it hurt you if I move a bit?"

He slipped a strong arm beneath her shoulders and used it to support her as he smoothly flipped them over, so she was on top. "No, sparrow. You will not hurt me. Enjoy yourself however you wish. Only, let me hold you while you do. That is what Vithii men desire from knotting—the closeness of holding and caring for their female."

Rather than answer in words, she snuggled down against his hard-muscled body, wrapping herself around him and resting with her head tucked neatly under his chin. His strong arms came up and enfolded her, a bulwark of protection between her and the world outside that seemed so intent on killing them both. She breathed him in, feeling safe and at peace for the first time since forever.

The intoxicating buzz of pleasure she couldn't escape formed a pulsing counterpoint to her newfound serenity. And why would any woman in their right mind *want* to escape this? Tentatively, she flexed her hips, still worried about making him uncomfortable despite his dismissal of her concerns.

He only hummed in contentment, though, sliding one large hand up and down the length of her back in a lazy caress. Reassured, she did it again—little rolling circles of her hips that pressed his knot against her G-spot and her clit against his pelvis. Inside, the clever little tip of his cock worried at the neck of her womb, teasing it.

It sort of made sense, she supposed—a tight knot to keep his seed from leaking out, and a prehensile tip to stimulate the cervix, opening the way into the uterus, and to the egg beyond. Just coincidence, really, that the net effect for a human woman was to be plugged into continuous, unavoidable stimulation for as long as his body wanted to keep her there.

She lay in his arms, shuddering every few minutes as she rode the crest of another slow, bone-deep release. Her body grew heavy in his embrace as time passed; her mind grew hazy, the pleasure taking on a dreamlike quality. Viscerally real and immediate in some ways… yet surreal at the same time.

The tattooed skin of his collarbone was salty under her lips. She latched onto it, only half aware, vaguely remembering the way he'd nipped his way down her body earlier. A deep hum of satisfaction resonated through his chest, and one of his hands came up to cradle her head, holding her in place.

It was obviously encouragement, so she bit down harder and sucked as the next climax washed over her. His taste grew coppery as the mark she had raised to the surface grew more livid.

Time was meaningless, measured only by the ebb and flow of her pleasure, but at some point, he began to speak, the words a low, soothing rumble under her cheek. He told her how he had been drawn to her from the first time he saw her, lying injured in the shuttle. He told her about the Vithii mating bond, and how he'd tried to fight it, and how utterly useless that attempt at resistance had been.

He told her all the ways he admired her. Told her how brave she was, how beautiful. How noble.

The words spilled from him as though he were barely aware that he was speaking aloud. At any other time, in any other place than curled here in his arms, she might have been able to dismiss them, because they were so completely at odds with how she had always seen herself. But, here and now, how could she possibly ignore them?

A powerful and dangerous Vithii fugitive loved her, and she loved him back. Now, they just had to stay alive long enough to do something about it.

Hunter held his human mate. The wash of hormones and endorphins pouring through his veins loosened his tongue, as it always seemed to do for Vithii males. It didn't matter, though. There was nothing he desired, at this moment, to hide from the woman sprawled across his chest.

She was finally succumbing to exhaustion after almost a full cycle spent writhing against his knot with tiny, barely-there movements which nonetheless appeared to give her considerable pleasure. Almost as much pleasure, he suspected, as he had gained from watching her and feeling her in his arms.

He could feel himself beginning to soften inside her. In more relaxed circumstances, he might have lasted longer, but she seemed to be well satisfied, regardless. She was going boneless against him now, growing heavy and pliant.

"Do Vithii really not kiss?" she murmured against his skin, the words slurring a bit. "Is that true?"

"Vithii bite," he told her. "We mark each other, to stake our claim. Though... I tried not to leave marks on you, earlier." In fact, he'd been rather proud of his restraint. To say that it hadn't come easily would be a considerable understatement.

"You could've done," she said, sounding more than half asleep. "I left one on you, I think. Tell you what... if we survive, you can mark me all you want, and I'll teach you how humans kiss. That'll be like... our reward..."

With those final words, she fell asleep, her breath evening out. He continued to hold her until his cock slipped free of her warm, welcoming passage. She made a discontented noise, but did not wake—not even when he maneuvered her limbs so he could hook the tangled blanket from the foot of the bed and drag it over them.

"Lights off," he said, pitching his voice low.

Possibly, Skye would have preferred to go take a shower before settling in for the remainder of the night. However, he was loath to wake her when she finally seemed to be sleeping peacefully. In fact, he was a little tired now himself. Perhaps he would doze for a while, before checking on things in the lab.

Just for a bit...

A knock on the door startled him into wakefulness. After a bare instant of disorientation, memory returned and his eyes sought out the chrono on the wall. It was not yet dawn. Skye was still wrapped around him, asleep, though she'd slid down at some point and was now curled against his side rather than draped on top of him.

Before he could organize his thoughts against the protective instincts urging him to snarl at whoever was outside the room until they left, the door slid open.

Apparently, he'd been too distracted to engage the privacy lock last night.

He tensed, unable to override his body's reaction to the idea of another male entering his female's den. Fortunately, the others hadn't been quite *that* stupid.

"Lights, twenty percent," said Ryder.

"What's wrong?" he asked, pitching his voice low.

Ryder held her features very still. In the low light, he could not parse her expression. "Sorry to intrude in your little love nest," she said. "You need to get some clothes on and get out here. Ash is on the comm. He has news."

SIXTEEN

Skye stumbled out of the bedroom behind Hunter a couple of minutes later, with no underwear beneath her jumpsuit and almost certainly reeking of sex. It was amazing how the prospect of imminent genocide put little things like modesty and personal humiliation in perspective.

At any other time in her life, she would have been appalled at the idea of a bunch of people knowing that she'd just spent the night having wildly inappropriate sex with a man she'd only met days ago. Now, what did it truly matter? Even if Ryder and Kade *were* looking at her with some variation of disapproval, anger, or both. At least Pax and Draven were doing a better job of keeping their opinions on the matter hidden.

Not that it was any of their business. Besides, they all had far more important things to worry about.

Hunter wasted no time in crossing to the comm unit. She followed him. It was broadcasting voice only, and the audio quality was poor.

"*Leetha*," Hunter said into the mic. "You have news."

Static crackled, Ash's voice emerging from beneath it. "I do. How is the project coming?" Even with the low quality of the transmission, he sounded exhausted.

"We need another thirty cycles or so," Ryder said, and Hunter relayed the answer.

"Good." A small burst of static obscured his voice for a moment. "—be just about in time."

"Say again, *leetha*," Hunter prompted. "We didn't copy that."

"I said, that should be just about in time. Things are moving on this end."

A cold fist gripped Skye's heart, driving out the last of the serenity she'd gained while curled in Hunter's arms.

Ash continued, "Also, the bird-catcher knows that a sparrow escaped his net last week. And he has a suspicion about what that sparrow might have been carrying. He's taking appropriate measures in response."

"Not unexpected, I suppose," Hunter said. "Are you safe?"

"Define *safe*," Ash said, still sounding tired. "Look, I need to get off of here before the scanners cycle back to check this frequency. I'll be at Location Four by this evening, and that's where I plan to ride this thing out. I've had the new speakers delivered there, since they might come in handy for the big party. Let me know if you need me."

The communication cut off abruptly.

"I got some of that," Skye said. "I gather the Premiere knows I escaped with the antidote? And he's planning on releasing the bio-agent soon?"

"Yeah," Draven said. "Ash was also saying that he'll be at one of Kade's hideouts after this evening—Location Four, of the seven we have set up right now. He's got some heavy duty transmission equipment with him, in case we need to hijack a media signal during the operation to get a message out to the public."

She nodded, aware that a lot more had been going on behind the scenes than she was aware of.

Hunter turned to Kade. "When can we move?"

"Ryder says thirty cycles for the antidote to be ready, but I need thirty-six for that tech I told you about," Kade said.

"And this tech is vital?"

"If you want to change this from a stone-cold suicide mission to a mission that is merely stupid and reckless, then, in my opinion, the tech is vital."

Hunter gave a single, sharp nod. "Then we move in thirty-six cycles. Is the tanker coming to us, or are we taking the bots to the tanker?"

"We're going to them," Pax said. "Jago uses unmarked hovervans for transporting his drugs. We'll go in two teams, each with one van. That doubles our chances of at least one team making it. The tanker is scheduled to arrive at the water treatment plant at oh-seven-hundred. We can make the switch under cover of darkness, but we'll have to hunker down at the depot until morning."

"Better to have some slack in the timeline in case things don't go to plan," Hunter said. "Ash made it sound like security at the water plant might be heightened, but I'll be surprised if they tighten things down within the privately owned support industries."

Kade nodded. "Agreed. The tanker crew doesn't care what we're doing with their truck. They only care that they'll be getting enough money to retire and move to one of the ring worlds."

"Good." Hunter surveyed them all, his gaze lingering for a moment on each of them. "You all know what to do. Get some food, and some rest if you haven't had any. We'll convene in the break room in three cycles to study the layout of the treatment plant in more detail."

The others grunted or nodded in acknowledgement, already scattering to start their tasks or grab a bit of rest. Hunter remained sitting at the chair next to the comm unit, obviously preoccupied. When they were alone, Skye placed a hand on his shoulder.

"I'm going to take a shower and prep some meals for anyone who needs them," she said. "I'll meet you in the break room with the others."

She'd been braced for distance—for him to pull back, perhaps even pretend nothing had happened between them. It was a huge relief when, instead, he looked up at her and lifted her hand from his shoulder to his lips, brushing a light, nipping caress of teeth over the backs of her knuckles.

"Of course, sparrow," he said. "I'm sorry your rest was interrupted, but then again, it's good to finally have a plan in place."

She tried to smile. "Yes. At least we're moving now."

He let her hand slip free, and she went to have a quick wash before she could be tempted to try and drag him back to the questionable haven of her borrowed bed.

<hr>

The next thirty-six cycles dragged, while at the same time seeming hectic. Ryder and Pax were busy triple-checking the failsafe programming on the nanotech. The last thing they needed after releasing actively reproducing bots into an uncontrolled environment was for the damned things to malfunction and start multiplying out of control, breaking down all the raw materials in their path in an unstoppable cascade of destruction.

Meanwhile, Draven was isolating the first samples of bot-produced antitoxin for quality checks. Skye, Hunter, and Kade hovered over him as he peered through a microscope at a slide of human tissue culture.

"It's working," he said with relief. "It's blocking the cell receptors so the toxin can't latch on—at least, it's blocking them under *in vitro* conditions."

Skye took a deep breath, aware that she could finally contribute something.

"Great," she said. "I guess you'll be needing a volunteer for a quick and dirty clinical trial, in that case. Someone get me a glass of water with the expected concentration of antidote in it, and lets see how it does under real world conditions."

"No," Hunter said immediately.

She looked at him. "Don't be stupid. We can't exactly release it into the water supply without testing it on someone first. Ash is the only other human you've got, and he's conspicuously *not here* right now."

"She's right," Kade said, somewhat to Skye's surprise.

"You will *not* do this," Hunter growled.

Skye turned, glaring up at him. "I wasn't asking your *permission*. There are thousands of lives at stake. Tens of thousands. And if the antidote doesn't work, I'll be in just as much danger as they will when the Premiere starts releasing the bioagent into the atmosphere."

Hunter's fists clenched, but he didn't try to rebut her argument. Kade looked between the two of them, still with the sour expression that he'd worn since shortly after they'd arrived. "Go see Ryder," he told her. His eyes slid back to Hunter, uncompromising. "We'll stay here and wait for you. In case it's not clear, *tei'laal*, I'm exercising the privileges we agreed to in our earlier discussion."

When it became apparent that Hunter would not try to physically force his way past Kade and stop her, she tore her eyes away from his tense form and hurried out of the room to find the medic. Ryder listened to her offer with a neutral expression.

"All right," she said. "If you're willing to risk it, I'll dose you and then inject you with a sample of the toxin. Do me a favor and don't fucking die, though. Because if you do, Hunter will try to tear my head off my shoulders."

She didn't appear to be joking, and Skye finally began to understand the others' less than enthusiastic reaction to finding out Hunter had mated her. Apparently, it wasn't just a matter of them sleeping together. This was something… *more*. She had a feeling there were many things she didn't understand yet, but this was hardly the time for personal issues.

First, they had to survive the next couple of days.

The antitoxin was completely undetectable in the water Skye drank. A little while later, Ryder injected her with a concentrated sample of the toxin produced by her father's bio-agent, and kept her under observation for a couple of cycles. She felt terribly queasy for a bit, and her head started ach ing with a dull throb centered behind her left eye, but that was the extent of it.

"You did it, Ryder," Skye told her, feeling crappy and ill, but *alive*. "You, and Pax, and Draven *did it*."

"Let's not break out the celebratory booze just yet," the gruff woman shot back. "For now, I'll just content myself with the fact that Hunter won't be coming after me, packing a blaster set on full."

In fact, when she found him, Hunter was pacing the length of the break room, while Kade and Pax studied the hologram of the treatment plant. He whirled when she walked through the door, tension in every line of his body.

"It's not the most fun I've ever had," she said, "but it works. We have a functioning antitoxin that appears to be effective at low dosages delivered orally."

"Good," Pax said, and Kade nodded in satisfaction.

Hunter's hands closed around her shoulders, gripping convulsively. She smiled up at him despite her pounding head. "Don't look like that," she told him. "I'm fine. Now, tell me what I missed."

"Mostly," said Pax, "you missed him trying to wear a hole through the floor. But I think we've got a good idea of the way water travels through the system, now. There are only two system-wide shutoff points downstream of the reservoir where we'll be pumping in the contents of the tanker, here and here." He pointed, his finger passing through the blue light of the 3-D construction plans. "We estimate that a critical mass of bots and antidote will have passed through the last shutoff valve within six cycles of being introduced to the reservoir."

"Six cycles?" she asked, taken aback. "That's… an awfully long time. What happens if the authorities get wind of what we're doing before then?"

"Things get ugly," Kade said simply.

"With luck," Hunter said, apparently ready now to rejoin their regularly scheduled conversation, "we'll be in and out without anyone suspecting a thing."

"*Luck*," Pax scoffed.

"Don't be like that, Pax," she said. "Surely we're due some luck, after all of this?"

"You meatbags never learn," he replied, shaking his head.

◆

The next bit of drama came not long before they were scheduled to leave. Jago had just sent over the hovervans. Skye, Kade, and Hunter were making final plans while the others loaded the materials and weapons for transport.

"How are you going to get me into the plant?" Skye asked, since no one had addressed that problem yet. "They'll be expecting a Vithii tanker crew. You'll have to hide me somehow."

"You won't be coming with us to the plant," Kade said without a flicker of expression. "I'm arranging private transport for you to Ash's position."

Stunned, she clenched her fists and walked forward until she was in his face, staring up at him. "The *fuck* I won't be."

"This isn't personal, Skye," Hunter said. "And it wasn't even my decision. There's no room for an untrained human civvy in a high-risk quasi-military operation like this. Your presence would put us all in additional danger."

She whirled on him, turning her back on Kade for the moment. "You think so? Give me your blaster." She stretched out her hand demandingly, palm-up, not breaking eye contact.

Kade snorted behind her. "Planning on taking us hostage and demanding to come along for the ride?"

She didn't turn to look at him. "I'm planning on showing you why you shouldn't make assumptions regarding things you don't know shit about." She gestured with her open palm. "Hunter. *Blaster.*"

Hunter was frowning at her in consternation, but when she didn't back down, he slowly un-holstered his weapon and handed it to her, grip first. She examined the blaster with a quick flick of her eyes—an unfamiliar make, but a fairly standard design. She dialed the beam from wide dispersion to narrow, and the intensity to low.

"Neither Temple nor I could figure out a way to smuggle weapons into the heart of the Regime's compound," she began, checking the blaster's sights. "Because of that, I had to stand there like a cornered rabbit and watch my father die without lifting a finger to save him… or to avenge him."

Both men were looking at her intently, now.

"But Daddy made sure that when we were growing up, my brother and I learned how to take care of ourselves. He taught us how to fly shuttles and hoppers. He made us learn basic self-defense."

She looked around, and saw a safety notice—written in Standard—hanging on the wall at the far end of the large, echoing lab. "He also taught us how to shoot. And when the Vithii started passing laws restricting humans from owning weapons, we kept in practice by going to those stupid laser-tag alleys, taking out mid-level business managers and corporate execs doing team-building exercises."

Hunter and Kade were still staring at her like she'd grown a second head. Her mouth twisted in irritation. "Keep your eye on the safety poster over there. Specifically, the letter 'o' in the word 'caution'."

With that, she lifted the heavy blaster, settling in a classic firing stance with her free hand wrapped around her firing wrist, steadying her aim. She breathed out, going still and silent, then let off six shots in rapid succession. When the smoke of burning plastic and paint cleared, the last three letters of 'caution' were obliterated.

"Well, then," Kade said.

Hunter looked from her, to the warning poster, and back to her again. After a heavy pause, he said, "Shooting at a person is a completely different thing than shooting at a piece of plastic hanging on a wall. Are you telling me that you wouldn't flinch at the idea of killing someone, little sparrow?"

"Killing Regime guards, you mean?" she said, hearing cold hatred seep into her voice. *Fucking try me.*"

"We needn't bloody her hands, Hunter," Kade said. "We have weapons with stun settings."

Hunter's eyes flew to Kade, disbelieving. "You're not actually considering this."

"I'm doing more than considering it. She'll be an asset, so she's coming."

"Damn straight I am," Skye said, her voice still cold with anger.

"And if I forbid it?" Hunter asked, his tone dangerous.

SEVENTEEN

Kade's voice remained level. Cold. "Then we'll ask the others, who will agree with me. And that won't do any favors for morale, or those team dynamics you were so concerned about when we spoke a few days ago."

Hunter ground his teeth, hating every aspect of what was happening. His entire life had been defined by making the smart decision, the right decision, independent of any feelings he might have on the matter. It was what had allowed him, as a youngster, to abandon the two women who had treated him as a son, leaving one of them dead, and the other one dying, as he fled to protect his own life.

Where had that dispassion gone? Where was his cold decision making ability now?

It had vanished, lost somewhere inside a slender human accountant with gold hair and flashing, angry blue eyes. But Kade had him in a corner, and he knew it. Hunter could not afford to have the others start questioning his leadership or his decisions on the cusp of such an important operation. Frustration surged, but he swallowed it in a single, bitter gulp.

"Do what you will," he grated, because he knew that they were *going* to do it, whether he agreed or not.

"Right," Skye said. "I'm probably skinny enough to lie under a dark blanket in the footwell of the tanker cab. There's no reason why they'd check, is there?"

"Depends on how paranoid they're being," said Kade. "But if they do check the cab, it will most likely be with a scanner. I've got jammers that can block your life signs against something like that."

Already, events were moving forward without him. "Take every possible precaution, Kade," he said. "And I need to speak to you privately before you join the others to help with the loading."

Kade gave a wary nod. Skye handed Hunter his blaster, her face still alight with righteous indignation.

"I'll leave you both to it, then," she said, and left to help the others.

When she was gone, his closest friend looked at him with a closed-off expression.

"I know when I've been out-maneuvered," Hunter said grimly, and Kade's tense stance relaxed by a fraction. "But I have a request to make, not as the leader of this mission, but as your brother-in-arms. Your *tei'laal*."

Only someone who knew Kade well could have seen the way his hard gray eyes softened.

"Then make it, Hunter," he said. "When you're done, I have a request to make of you, as well."

Shortly after dawn, Skye found herself lying amongst a pile of weapons in the rear footwell of a grimy old tanker cab, being smothered by a heavy black cloth. The floor under her was covered in a layer of old grit, and the interior of the truck smelled of grease and stale Vithii sweat. Hunter's heavy boots jabbed into her shoulder, Pax's into her thighs.

The pair had been relegated to the back seat, caps pulled down low to put their faces in shadow, hopefully hiding Pax's metal implants and Hunter's distinctive tattoos from casual observation. Draven—the least likely of them to draw attention—was driving, with Ryder and Kade sitting next to him along the front bench seat.

Hunter muttered a time-check, the words muffled by the blanket covering her, and Pax answered. It was coming up on oh-seven-hundred. They must be close.

Moments later, the truck pulled to a stop, brakes screeching. "We're here," Hunter murmured, barely audible—no doubt for her benefit.

The others were wearing uniforms borrowed from the bribed tanker crew. Skye still wore the black jumpsuit Hunter had acquired for her. She had braided her hair tightly to keep it out of her way, tucking it under the black balaclava they'd dug up for her from gods-knew-where. She was clutching the slender stun-blaster Kade had found for her against her chest. A second, more powerful blaster was holstered at her hip.

Considering that the plan was to casually drive in past the front gate and pump the contents of the tank they were hauling into the water system without raising suspicion, Kade certainly seemed to have brought along a small arsenal of weapons and tech. Most of which was currently poking and prodding her in all the wrong places as she shared the cramped space on the truck's floorboards with the deadly stash.

In addition, in the area between the cab and the tank designed to hold tools needed by the delivery crew, they had strapped a much larger piece of machinery. Skye was more than a bit awestruck to discover that the thing was a matter transportation unit—a highly experimental device that must have cost far more to acquire than Skye had earned cumulatively in her lifetime.

She'd had no idea matter transport units that large even *existed*. Both her father and Temple had occasionally waxed poetic about the new technology over the past couple of years, but they were talking about tiny units designed for small-scale experimentation. This one was *industrial*.

"Riskier than pumping the bots and antidote out of the tanker the old fashioned way," Kade had said, "but also considerably faster. This hunk of tech is our first backup plan if things start to go south during the offloading process."

The tanker crept forward, only to stop again. This time, Skye heard voices from outside as Draven lowered the window and spoke—presumably—with the treatment plant's gate security.

"We'll have to scan the cab," said one of the guards. "Where's the usual crew, anyway? I don't recognize you lot."

"Vinn and Grennie are out sick," Draven said. "The supervisor had to shuffle everyone else around to cover all the deliveries this morning. What's with the scan, though? That's new. Something going on?"

"Nothing you need to worry about," said the guard. "Hang on, this'll just take a minute—"

There was a bit of muttering she couldn't make out. It seemed to take a hell of a lot longer than *a minute*.

"Problem?" Draven asked, impatience slipping into his tone. "We're on a tight schedule here."

"These readings are whacked. Fuckin' piece of shit scanner's playing up—"

More muttering.

"Look," said Draven, "why don't you just take a look for yourselves, so we can get this delivery offloaded and get back in time to load up the next shipment. We've got nothing to hide—"

Skye had to swallow the bubble of hysterical laughter that tried to choke its way free.

"—we just need to stay on schedule or the boss is gonna rip us a new one."

A pause, before the guard spoke again.

"Yeah. Yeah, okay."

The driver's side door opened at the front of the truck's cab. Skye held her breath, forcing all of her muscles to relax under the flimsy cover of the black cloth.

I am one with the footwell. I am one with the footwell. No human fugitives or piles of weapons down here... no sir. Just this dark, empty, boring space where people stick their feet. Move along, now—nothing to see here.

"Look, this all seems fine." The guard again. "Go on ahead. They're waiting for you at the coagulant tanks, as per usual."

"Sure thing," Draven said.

Skye's lungs were burning, but she didn't let out her breath until the driver's door had slammed shut and the truck was moving. They were in. They'd made it. She felt suddenly shaky.

Maybe, she thought, *this is going to go off without a hitch, after all.*

Hunter kept his head down in the back seat as Draven maneuvered the tanker alongside a large storage unit. This, he knew, was where the poly-electrolyte solution they *should* have been carrying was kept, in readiness for mixing with untreated water before heading to the flocculation basin.

Hopefully, they would be able to offload the tanker's contents into the storage tank before anyone raised the alarm. Once they did, however, they had to throw open the main valve that would drain the nanotech and antidote into the water supply as quickly as possible, rather than the usual slow drip feed.

At that point, they'd have to neutralize any employees who were unlucky enough to be present, to prevent them raising the alarm. Of course, it wouldn't take long for automated sensors to pick up on the irregularity in the system, regardless.

The bribed tanker crew had walked them through the usual process of offloading. Normally, they worked in crews of four, so Pax—the most conspicuous with his cyborg implants—melted back into the shadows of the truck's cab while Hunter, Kade, Ryder, and Draven exited to hook up the delivery line and start pumping.

Hunter let Kade and Draven do the talking, knowing it was best for him to remain as much in the background as possible. He tried not to worry about Skye, still huddled in the back of the truck.

Pax was with her. And she was, quite literally, surrounded by weapons.

Kade had already activated the vid-feed jammer as he stepped out of the truck, so the cameras in this part of the plant should be out of commission. Again, a calculated risk, since the malfunction might draw attention. The four of them worked with the two plant employees to tighten the hose connection between the tanker and the storage unit. When it was ready, Hunter turned on the pump. Bots and antidote started flowing into the storage tank.

The process would take about twenty minutes. After that, another half-cycle to overpower the employees, open the main valve, and let the storage tank's contents drain into the water supply. Then, Ryder estimated four to five cycles before a critical mass of bots—along with the antidote they were churning out at the microscopic level—made it past the final shut-off point. After that, it would be loose in the Capital's water supply, and beyond anyone's power to stop.

If they were lucky enough to get the contents of the storage tank dumped into the main basin and return everything to normal settings without being discovered, they planned to throw the unconscious employees in the tanker and drive out like nothing had happened.

If, on the other hand, someone raised the alarm before they could get out, they'd have to hunker down and defend the area until the bots were loose in the system, preventing anyone from shutting off the last-ditch containment valve. Hunter knew which scenario he'd bet on, if he were a betting man.

Draven was chatting with the two employees, doing his best to keep them distracted. Hunter strolled casually behind the tanker, and glanced in the windows of the truck cab to reassure himself that Skye and Pax weren't easily visible. They weren't, so he went to double-check Kade's matter transport tech and power it on, just in case.

He had barely flicked the main power switch when distant alarms wailed into life.

"What the fuck?" one of the employees asked, only to fall to the ground a moment later with a choked gurgle, as Draven knocked him out with a sharp blow to the back of the head.

The other employee hared off, shouting for help. Unfortunately for him, his chosen escape route took him right past Hunter's spot behind the tanker. Hunter lunged at him, grabbing him by one sleeve and whirling him around. The man was big, but obviously not a fighter—he tried to jerk free, but Hunter effortlessly tripped him and caught him in a half-nelson, pressing stiff fingers into the nerve clusters at the base of his neck until he went limp and flopped to the ground.

"The vid-feed jammer must have tipped them off," Kade said. He was already climbing up to reach the controls of the matter transport unit. "Ryder, Draven—throw the transporter's receiving pad into the main water basin. And someone open the top hatch on this tank. Then all of you need to stand well clear."

Hunter was still near the truck, so he scrambled up the ladder on the side of the tanker. The large access hatch at the top was stiff and heavy, but he threw his weight against the locking wheel. It creaked and spun reluctantly, undogging the hatch so Hunter could throw it open, hinges squeaking.

He slid down the ladder and backed away, aware that Pax and Skye had joined them, and were handing out weapons. Hunter accepted two blasters and a stun wand, just as a whine rose from the transport unit. It grew in pitch and intensity until, a few moments later, the entire tank started to glow and dissolve into whirling sparkles.

Hunter felt a breeze blow past, rushing to fill the void left by the metal tank and its precious contents. The hose connected to the storage unit flopped to the ground, cut off raggedly where the matter transport field ended. Almost simultaneously, an eerie glow lit the bottom of the reservoir where the others had dropped the receiving pad, as the tanker materialized beneath the surface. A wave of displaced water sloshed up, followed by huge bubbles as the air inside the partially emptied tank escaped through the open access hatch. Water would be rushing in to replace it, Hunter knew, mixing with the remaining slurry of bots and antidote.

A few moments later, all was still and quiet again.

Pax and Ryder moved without prompting to open the valve and release the contents of the polyelectrolyte storage unit into the water basin as well.

"Is the truck still drivable?" Hunter asked. "We didn't transport any vital components by accident?"

Kade hopped down from the area at the back of the cab, where the matter transport controls were mounted. "Nope," he said, "just the tank."

Hunter nodded. "Everybody inside, in that case. Draven, drive around to the other side of the reservoir. We'll use the truck as a partial barricade, to help defend the shut-off valve. On-site security will be here any minute."

They were banking on the fact that the Regime could not afford to destroy any important components of the treatment plant while attacking their position. The Capital needed water, and without the treatment plant, there wasn't any. So they couldn't simply drop a bomb on the place, or even use any heavy artillery as long as Hunter and the others stood behind things that could be destroyed accidentally.

They piled into the truck cab. The engine roared to life, and Draven put his foot down, scattering the first arriving guards like startled birds. This was plant security; it would take a bit for Regime troops to arrive on site. One of the men managed to get off a blaster shot. A sharp popping noise echoed through the cab. The old tanker was ground transport with no hover capabilities, and the way it suddenly swerved to one side let them know he'd managed to puncture a tire.

Draven clamped his jaw and steered into the skid, slowing just enough to get the rig under control and continue, driving on the shredded tire. The security guards fell behind, chasing them on foot. The reservoir that held the water after it drained through the gravity-fed filtration basin was huge. They gained a good bit of distance on their pursuers by the time they reached the giant collection pipes at the far end.

Fortunately, the old construction plans Ash had stolen for them were surprisingly accurate. Draven hit the brakes, positioning the truck in the spot they'd decided earlier would make for the best defensive positioning. Sparks flew from the bare metal wheel rim as it ground to a halt. A single frightened employee scurried out of their way and ran as fast as she could in the other direction.

Hunter ignored her. He already had the passenger door open, barking orders as he jumped down. "Pax. Ryder. Skye. Find some cover and take out the security guards as they approach. Draven and Kade, help me get the cutting torch set up. Let's try to make it as difficult as possible for anyone to use this shutoff valve."

Draven hauled the cutting torch over to Hunter. The water pipe was huge—if he and Draven stood on opposite sides and reached for each other, they could not have touched fingers. The wheel controlling the shutoff valve was nearly two meters in diameter, and almost certainly needed several people to turn. Fortunately, they had no interest in turning it. Quite the opposite.

He and the others slipped polarized goggles out of their pockets and donned them. Kade fired up the plasma torch, goggles darkening automatically against its blazing white tip. Hunter helped him steady it, and they used the cutter to melt through the base of the shutoff wheel, where it disappeared inside the pipe. They had to be extremely careful not to damage the pipe itself—but without the leverage of the wheel, it would take time and specialized machinery for anyone to successfully close the valve.

After several minutes of cutting, the sound of metal groaning under the strain assaulted their ears. The heavy wheel tilted, hanging suspended for several moments before shearing off and falling to the ground with a deafening clang.

It would take time for Regime forces to arrive, assess the situation, and move in on them. Now, though, the on-site guards were already closing on their position. A stun beam—from Ryder, as far as Hunter could tell—caught the lead guard in the neck. He fell like a sack of grain, and his comrades immediately dove for cover.

They had agreed ahead of time not to use lethal force on the paid security staff if at all avoidable. Once the Regime showed up, though, all bets were off. They would do whatever was required to defend their position.

Loudspeakers crackled into life. "*Attention all employees. Attention all employees,*" said a female Vithii voice. "*This is an emergency situation. Lock down all stations and proceed to the nearest safe area. This is not a drill.*"

"Help me get the matter transport unit unstrapped from the truck and behind cover before things start to get too exciting," Kade said. "The fucking thing cost an arm and a leg—I don't want it to get so much as scratched."

Hunter shot him a look. "I'm not entirely certain about your priorities sometimes, Kade," he said, hurrying to help him nonetheless, while Draven covered them.

A lucky blaster shot from one of the security guards exploded against the cab of the truck, showering them with sparks and bits of burning metal.

"Did anyone bother to brief these grunts on the part where they're not supposed to risk damaging the water supply system by shooting at it?" Draven wondered aloud as they dragged the transporter's control unit and dispersal pad behind the shelter of the massive water pipe.

Another shot ricocheted off a nearby support beam. "Apparently not," Hunter said. "Hopefully their aim's not good enough to do any real damage."

The others were crouched behind concrete pillars and whatever other solid objects were handy. Hunter, Kade, and Draven slipped over to join them during a lull in the onslaught of blaster fire. A guard about forty meters from their position popped his head up while they were moving, readying his blaster for a shot. Skye and Kade fired simultaneously, both stun beams converging on the unlucky security grunt and throwing him backward to the ground under their combined power.

Draven winced. "Ouch. That's gonna hurt," he said.

Hunter took cover next to Skye, unable to keep from giving her a careful once over to make sure she was unharmed. She was fine, of course—though that might not remain the case once the serious firepower arrived. The idea of her being in this kind of danger was still a punch to the gut, and he berated himself for letting it distract him when he needed to be on his best game.

EIGHTEEN

For now, Skye was all right. Better than all right. She was magnificent—crouched behind their pillar, motionless as a stalking predator, stun weapon held at the ready. As he watched, she leaned out once more to fire off a quick shot, darting back before the guards could target her.

Hunter tore his gaze away from her by an act of will, forcing himself back to practicalities.

"Regime forces may arrive at any time. Everyone don ear and eye protection," he ordered. He glanced around a moment later, making sure everyone was kitted out. "Mic check."

"Check," said Kade.

"Check." Skye, that time.

The others checked in, one by one. Hunter confirmed reception, and opened a private channel. "Kade, you good?"

There was a short hesitation. "Yeah, I'm good for another couple of cycles, at least. I'll let you know."

"You do that," Hunter said, and cut the connection.

Normally, Kade was defensive as fuck about his ability to remain self-sufficient despite his neurotonin addiction—nearly to the point of obsession. Yesterday, though, after the two of them had fought about Skye's inclusion in the mission, Kade made an unprecedented request of him.

"I need you to do something for me," he'd said. "Prophets only know how long this mission will drag on, especially if we end up pinned down, defending our position against Regime troops. I need you to hold a few doses of neurotonin for me, so I'll have it if I need it, and won't be tempted to do anything stupid."

One of the curses of Kade's addiction was that when withdrawal started and his mental acuity began to slip, the cravings made the desire to overdose almost impossible to resist. If he had multiple doses on his person, he might easily be compelled to inject all of them—a mistake that would probably be fatal.

For all the years Hunter had known him, Kade had carefully arranged his life around his addiction, stashing additional doses in his ship or some other location using a time-released container that would only open when he was due for another shot. He couldn't even trust himself to carry such a secured container around with him, though. With his extensive knowledge of mechanics and electronics, he would almost certainly be able to circumvent or destroy the mechanism if he got it into his head to do so.

It had long been a source of frustration to the others that Kade would not simply rely on one of them to carry additional doses for him and hand them over as needed. But the mere suggestion that he needed such help from them had always been enough to throw him into a cold rage.

Until now.

Today, Hunter was carrying four of the precious doses in a padded pouch, hidden inside his borrowed workmen's coveralls. He knew Kade had injected himself right before they'd left the tanker depot, early that morning. So he should, in fact, be all right for two or three more cycles, as he had claimed. They would just have to hope that, two or three cycles from now, they'd still be in one piece, so he could inject the next dose and buy himself another short stretch of life.

A new voice came over the loudspeaker. Male. Cold. "*Attention, saboteurs. Put down your weapons and come into the open. Lie face down on the ground, and you will not be harmed.*"

Draven snorted. "Yeah, right. Because that's gonna happen."

"Which part?" Ryder asked. "The *putting down your weapons* part or the *will not be harmed* part?"

"Both," Draven said, still darkly amused.

"Seriously. Has that line *ever* worked in the history, of, well… *ever?*" said Skye.

She was nervous. Frightened. Hunter could smell it on her; sense it rolling off of her in waves. But she didn't let it stop her. She still crouched behind the pillar, peeking out to look for targets, cracking wise-ass jokes like the hardened criminal that she so obviously wasn't. Even if he hadn't fallen for her, he still would have admired her.

"It certainly won't be working today," he said, indulging himself by resting a hand on the tense line of her shoulder for a bare instant. She glanced up at him with those bright blue eyes, flashing him a brief, grim smile before returning her attention to the remaining guards.

"Damn right, it won't," she agreed, and fired off another shot.

Skye jerked back behind the pillar she was sharing with Hunter as return fire sizzled past. On some distant level, she was terrified out of her skin. What if they couldn't defend the shut-off valve for a sufficient stretch of time? What if the Regime managed to close it before enough bots had escaped, and everything they'd worked for was for nothing? It was almost worse, knowing that she was the only human in the city that had taken the antidote. The only one safe from the bio-weapon.

Of course, if she failed, it would hopefully mean she was already dead. Because the alternative would be capture, and that really *would* be the end of her.

She didn't think the others were any more eager to end up in a Regime cell than she was, which was comfort of a sort. Hunter's one-man mission of vengeance aside, she couldn't really claim to understand why the others seemed willing to risk their lives to help her save the humans on Ilarius. Yet she owed them everything—this strange, dysfunctional family of misfits and undesirables.

There was no way she could see for them to get out of this situation unscathed, now that they'd been discovered. She spared a thought for Ash, holed up with his transmission equipment at an undisclosed location. Would he manage to escape, only to find himself the only surviving member of the Shadow Wing?

For some reason, *that* was the thing that brought the sting of tears behind her eyes and a lump to her throat. She swallowed everything back, and tried to focus on the here-and-now. On their goal.

The loudspeakers flared to life again with a squeal. *"Attention, saboteurs. Law enforcement is closing on your position. Surrender yourselves now. This is your final opportunity."*

Kade's voice muttered over the commlink in her ear. "Nice of them to warn us."

"Very thoughtful," Draven agreed. "I feel all warm and fuzzy now."

Skye checked her goggles and ear protection one more time, knowing that things were going to get a lot more intense soon. The on-site security was armed with standard personal sidearms, but the Regime forces would be bringing bigger toys along with them.

Some things, they could defend against, and some, they would be powerless against. But the others had agreed that flash bombs and stun grenades would be the likely first line of attack, since they wouldn't damage the plant's infrastructure. Hence the necessity for the auto-adjusting goggles and selective hearing protection. Both devices would react instantaneously to light and noise over a certain threshold, blocking it.

In addition to his blaster, Kade was holding a portable hand-scanner. "Fifteen vehicles approaching," he reported. "I'm getting quite a bit of interference from all of the metal pipes in here, but it looks like maybe forty or fifty troops on board. Of course, that'll just be the first wave."

Movement caught Skye's attention, and she loosed another stun blast across the distance separating them from the plant's security guards. She felt a vicious stab of satisfaction as another body collapsed limply to the ground, out of commission.

That's three notches for the gun belt. Wish you were here to see it, Temple.

"Troops approaching now," Kade reported, just as a small canister arced through the air and landed five or six meters away.

Hunter's bulk pressed her against the rough concrete pillar an instant before the flash-bang went off. She had a confused impression of blinding light followed immediately by dark, and an incredibly loud noise muffled as though it had occurred underwater. The sonic protection didn't prevent her from feeling like she'd been clapped on both ears by an immensely strong assailant, though, and she would have reeled if she weren't trapped between Hunter's hard-muscled torso and the pillar.

Nausea flooded her as the world tilted, her balance thrown off kilter by the concussion of sound waves. Something buzzed in her abused ears. It took several seconds for the noise to resolve into voices over the commlink, sounding strange and attenuated.

"Twelve units approaching at our two and ten o'clock." That was Kade, she thought dazedly. And how the hell could he sound so collected?

The darkness lifted as her goggles depolarized, but after-images still popped in her vision, and the world was spinning. Her stomach tried to rebel; she had to swallow hard several times to force its contents back down. Blaster beams sizzled through the air as the others targeted the approaching Regime troops.

She shook her head, trying to clear it, and checked that her stun weapon was still clutched in her clammy fingers.

"—Skye?" It was Hunter. From his tone, she didn't think it was the first time he'd called her name. "*Report*. Are you injured?"

She swallowed again, to make sure her voice would work when she tried to use it. "Just stunned, I think." She sounded odd to her own ears, like she was standing in a tunnel. "Are you and the others all right? Why didn't my ear protection work?"

His reply was grim. "Since you're not deaf, it *did* work. But we didn't take into account the difference between human and Vithii physical tolerance."

The old, familiar feeling of being weak, of not being good enough, crept through her. *No,* she thought. *No time for that. All that matters now is the mission.*

"I'll be all right," she said. "Let me up so I can shoot, damn it!"

Hunter eased his weight off of her, and she gripped the concrete post with one hand for balance.

"Keep your ear protection at maximum and rely on the commlink to communicate," he said, his voice starting to sound a bit clearer now. "It might help if you eliminate the lag time before the sound cancellation kicks in, tiny though it is."

"Right," she said, thumbing the little control pad nestled behind her right ear, and trying not to quail at the idea that more explosions like that would be coming.

It took longer than it should have to orient herself and figure out which directions were ten o'clock and two o'clock. When she did, she clenched her jaw and leaned hard against the pillar to ground herself and stabilize her aim. Fortunately, the others were already doing an admirable job of keeping the first troops from advancing.

She forced wavering vision to focus on the distant plasticrete barricade that the ones at two o'clock were using for shelter. Then she waited until a helmeted head appeared. Her first shot went comically wide, and her second shot missed by half a meter or so. The third one hit a guard squarely in the shoulder, though, and she frowned when he only staggered back a step, and righted himself.

"What the hell?" she asked. "My stunner isn't working. Is my power pack depleted?"

"They're wearing body armor," Hunter said tightly. "You'll have to hit a gap in it to take them down with a stun beam."

"Great," she said. She examined the next one who showed himself. Neck and chin were about the only option. Though she could maybe neutralize their effectiveness with an arm shot. It wouldn't knock them out, but if they couldn't lift that arm to hold a weapon, it was almost as good.

Her dizziness was giving way to a pounding headache, but at least that meant she could see straight. She peered around the opposite side of the pillar from where Hunter was aiming, focusing on the second group. Weapon held at the ready, she settled in for a pitched battle.

***

After what seemed like an eternity of fighting, Skye decided that siege warfare was the second worst thing she'd ever experienced, right behind watching her father die. Crashing a shuttle into a moon was a fucking beach vacation by comparison.

Draven was hurt, his left arm hanging useless by his side after one of the flash-bang grenades went off practically at his feet, throwing him to the ground. Mind you, he was still fighting, left hand tucked in the belt of his coveralls to keep the injured arm from flopping around while he fired off shot after shot with his right.

Skye felt like her ears were bleeding, and confusing afterimages seemed to be permanently tattooed on her retinas from stun grenade after stun grenade. It was getting harder each time to shake them off, and she knew with sick certainty that she wasn't pulling her weight in their defense anymore. Not by a long shot.

Kade's voice came over the commlink. "At some point, they're going to haul in more effective weapons. Gas grenades, for instance."

As if his actual words weren't worrying enough, she thought she could detect a familiar shakiness to his voice even with her abused eardrums. The suspicion was confirmed when Hunter replied, "It'll take a while for them to get authorization, and transport the weapons here from wherever they're stored. While we're waiting, it sounds like you'd better have another injection."

There was a lengthy pause. "Yeah, probably," Kade said. "Stay there. I'll come to you. Cover me, Pax?"

"Done," Pax rumbled, clearly in his element amongst the fierce fighting.

Kade had been sheltering between the shot-up hulk of the tanker truck and the pipe valve they were guarding. Pax laid down covering fire, and Kade darted out, running low as he crossed the distance between them. As he approached Skye and

Hunter's position, they turned to meet him. He slid to a halt, his eyes pinned on Skye's midsection.

She looked down at herself in confusion, not understanding what could have caught his attention in such a way. A red dot of light flickered crazily around her stomach and chest, like a silent, glowing insect. She stared at it stupidly for a beat, before several things happened in quick succession.

"*Shit!*" Kade cursed. "Sniper, six o'clock—"

Hunter's eyes had followed Kade's to the red light of the targeting laser, and tracked it back to its source. His mouth opened, and things seemed to slow down unnaturally as he lunged forward without a word. His body slammed into hers, driving the breath from her lungs as he shoved her violently to the side, sending her to the ground.

She hit hard, the light fabric of her jumpsuit doing little to protect her elbows and knees from the gritty concrete surface. She looked up, dazed. With her ear protection turned up to maximum, she couldn't hear a damn thing from the outside world. But Hunter was leaning against the pillar they'd been using for cover, one arm clutching the smoking patch of melted fabric and charred flesh in his side.

His teeth were bared in a rictus of pain, but he hadn't uttered a sound as he'd been shot. Skye's heart froze in her chest.

"*No!*" she screamed, scrabbling on stinging hands and knees to get to him. Three quick shots flew past their position—friendly fire, coming from the vicinity of the truck.

"Sniper's neutralized," Pax reported over the comms.

Skye barely registered the words in her desperation to get to Hunter and somehow *undo* the last few seconds by force of will alone. Hunter was sliding down the pillar in slow motion. A sob tried to claw its way up Skye's throat as she reached his side and clutched his shoulders, trying to keep him upright.

His attention was not on her, however, as he dragged in painful, rasping gulps of air. It was on Kade.

"Now, Kade," he grated, the words like sandpaper. "Get her… out… *now*."

Kade dropped to his knees on Hunter's other side as more blaster fire crackled around them. "You bastard son of a whore," he said in a voice gone strangely flat. "I will. Now, where is it? Where did you stash it?"

The noise that emerged from Hunter's throat could have been a cough or a bark of humorless laughter. "Left inside pocket. Sorry… *tei'laal*. Not looking good for either of us, is it?"

Kade pulled open the ruined fabric on the left side of Hunter's borrowed jumpsuit and cursed again.

"Hunter," Skye croaked, not recognizing her own voice.

His unfocused eyes turned in her direction, and he lifted a clumsy hand to press it to the side of her face. "Go, little sparrow," he said hoarsely. "Don't… worry about… me…"

She shook her head, not understanding. "What do you mean, *go*? I'm not going anywhere! Ryder, you need to *get over here*—"

Rough hands grabbed her and hauled her to her feet. She looked up at Kade's profile. At his clenched jaw. "What the hell are you doing! *Get off me*!" she yelled as he started to drag her away from Hunter, whose green eyes were sliding closed as he lost the fight to stay conscious.

"More covering fire, *now*," Kade snapped over the commlink, ignoring her as she jerked and struggled against his bruising hold.

The area lit up with weapons fire as he dragged her across the space between their two positions. Her attempt to get loose might have been the feeble fluttering of a trapped butterfly for all the notice he took of it.

"Stop!" she cried. Suddenly remembering her stun weapon, she reached for her belt—but she must have dropped it in the confusion of the sniper attack. "Kade, what are you *doing*! I thought he was your *friend*!"

The muscle in Kade's jaw twitched, but he did not reply—merely manhandled her toward the controls of the matter transport unit that they'd dragged under cover earlier.

"Hunter's down," he reported over the comms. "Hold this position at all costs. I'll return as soon as I can."

"What the fuck is *that* supposed to mean?" came Draven's reply.

"Kade. This is a poor tactical decision." Pax said.

"Tell me something I *don't* know," Kade said, sounding angry enough to spit nails. Without another word, he dragged Skye onto the transporter's dispersal pad.

The realization of what he intended finally penetrated her scrambled wits. She clenched the fist of her free arm and took a wild, desperate swing at his face. He batted it away effortlessly and shoved her back a step as a terrible itching, tickling feeling started to crawl over her flesh.

"No no *no*—" She tried to lunge sideways, off of the pad.

The world went dark, mid-leap.

NINETEEN

When Skye's surroundings sparkled into painful life again, she stumbled and collapsed in a heap, the breath driven from her lungs as her shoulder impacted roughly with the ground. Her stomach heaved, and she retched a thin stream of bile, curling into a fetal position against the horrible *wrongness* of the teleportation process.

The space was dim and grimy, illuminated by a single portable workman's light hanging in the corner. Through watering eyes, she saw Kade go down on one knee and empty the contents of his own stomach onto the dirty floor.

"*Fuck*," he said with feeling, wiping his mouth with the back of his sleeve. A moment later, he had her by the arm again and was dragging her up from the floor. She groaned, dry-retching at the sudden change in elevation.

"You bastard," she croaked, once she'd locked shaky knees enough to take her own weight. "If you had a way out, why didn't you take *him*?"

Kade was already dragging her forward, toward the side of the room where the single light was hanging, throwing a sickly yellow glow over everything. The place had the look of a disused basement—confirmed when he threw open a door to reveal stairs leading up.

"Because," he said, the tremor from earlier back in his voice, "the shit-for-brains made me vow to get you out if things started to fall to pieces." He met her eyes for the first time. "If he dies, that's on me. I was the one with the scanner, and I should have seen the sniper moving into position. But if the rest of them die because I'm not with them, that's on you. You and Hunter."

She jerked against his hold. "Fuck you!" she spat. "You could have stayed! We could have stayed!"

His eyes narrowed. "No. I couldn't."

Skye's rage boiled over. "And if you weren't a fucking *junkie* in withdrawal, you might have seen that sniper on the scanner and Hunter wouldn't have gotten shot in the first place!"

The grip on her arm tightened convulsively as the barb apparently hit home. "Right on all counts," Kade said. "If it makes you feel any better, Hunter was carrying my stash, and it was vaped by the blast that hit him. So I'm probably going to die right along with him today, in the most ugly and humiliating way possible."

As much as she might have wanted to spit the word *good* in his face, she couldn't. He was frog-marching her up the unlit staircase now, her feet stumbling and scrabbling on the steep steps.

"Where are we? What is this place?" she asked, trying to kick her brain into gear when all she wanted to do was collapse into a heap and sob. Or maybe scream, as she'd done into Hunter's broad chest the night her control had finally broken.

Kade's own control sounded like it was hanging by a thread. "It's Location Four. Where the fuck did you *think* it was?"

It took her a moment to put that together in her mind. "Wait," she said, "Ash is here?"

Kade didn't even bother to answer, but she imagined she could hear his teeth grinding together. Maybe Ash could talk Kade into taking her back to help fight, and saving Hunter instead. A tiny thread of hope wove through the horrible feeling of defeat filling her chest. She made more of an effort to force her shaky legs up step after step.

How many flights *were* there, anyway?

After an eternity of stubbing toes and cracking shins in the dark, Kade pushed open another door, this time into a deserted corridor thankfully lit by diluted sunlight filtering through dirty windows at the far end.

"Are there security cameras here?" Skye asked, suddenly worried that their presence might alert the authorities to the safehouse's location.

"Yes," Kade ground out, "but they're not hooked into the system."

"How can you be sure?" Skye demanded.

"I own the building," came the terse reply.

They fetched up in front of a door identical to every other door in the hallway. Kade rapped knuckles against the peeling paint with a complicated series of knocks and slapped his palm against the lock pad. It clicked and the door swung open.

Skye froze as they were confronted with the business end of a powerful phase rifle. Ash's deadly expression collapsed into relief as he recognized them, and he lowered the weapon. He was seated in a chair in front of a cobbled together control panel, and he looked awful—his face tinged gray and his body held carefully, as if he was in pain.

"Get inside and shut the door, Kade," he said. "What the hell are you doing here? This wasn't part of the plan."

"It was part of Hunter's plan," Kade said. "He's down for the count. Draven's injured, but functional."

Ash's dark brows drew together. "What about you two?"

"She's all right." Kade paused. "I'm in early-stage withdrawal. Hunter was holding doses for me, but they were destroyed when he was hit."

Skye spoke up. "Ash, you need to make him take me back and get Hunter out instead. I can still fight, and he'll *die* if he doesn't get help."

If he's not dead already. She quashed the terrible thought.

Sympathy flashed across Ash's features for only an instant before they hardened. "I've never been able to make either of the stubborn bastards do anything they don't want to do, Skye." His attention turned quickly to Kade. "Where do you need me—there, or here?"

Kade wavered for a bare moment before answering, "Here. She can't run the transmitting equipment, and even if I could stay functional long enough to do it, I'm Vithii. No reason for the humans to trust me."

Ash nodded. "Go on then. We'll be okay here."

"Ash, *please!*" Skye begged, finally succeeding in jerking free of Kade's grip.

"Look after her, *leetha*," said Kade, still ignoring her. "Hunter's orders."

"I'll do my best, Kade. Stay strong. We've got this end covered."

Kade left, closing the door behind him, even as Ash turned to her.

"*Ash*…" she said, hopelessness settling over her like a cloak once more.

He must have seen her start to waver before she even realized it was happening, because he rose from his chair with a poorly covered wince and crossed to take her shoulders. His grip was considerably less painful than the one Kade had employed to get her here. He steered her to a dusty chair in the corner just as her knees gave out.

She looked up at his dark eyes and bruised face. He regarded her in turn, the corners of his mouth turning down.

"Skye," he said, "this was never going to go down without casualties. You knew that. We all did. Something happened, though, didn't it. Between you and Hunter, I mean."

It wasn't phrased as a question, but Skye looked down at her lap and nodded, tears flooding her eyes.

"Shit," Ash whispered. "I'm sorry, sweetheart. Truly, I am. Even if I'm glad, in a way, that Hunter got a taste of that kind of love before it was too late."

A sob threatened to shake its way free of her chest. "I should be with him," she managed. "If we had to die, it should have been with us fighting together, side by side. Not with me hiding here like a coward."

"He wanted you safe," Ash said. "But that's not the important part. The important part is the mission. You can barely stand up. You wouldn't have been much help in holding the plant."

She winced, the painful truth hitting home. He continued, "But here, you can help. You're Zarian Chantrell's daughter. Not to mention the fact that studies have consistently shown humans respond better to female voices in times of emergency. I think we should start transmitting right away, and that you should read the statement—not me."

"Me?" she asked stupidly. "*Now?* I can barely string two words together. I can't even think—"

"Then pull yourself together," Ash said, uncompromising. "This has been your show from the very beginning. Now, we have to trust the others to hold the line, and worry about doing our part. We're so close, Skye. Don't fall apart on us now."

She swallowed hard. It was true. Hunter might be dying, but there were also tens of thousands of innocent people whose lives still hung in the balance. A horrible thought occurred to her.

"Ash," she said. "You haven't had the antidote yet. And… I don't have any with me."

The corners of his eyes crinkled in a brief smile. "That's all right. I won't need it, because there's a sink in the lav, and in a little while I can simply take a drink straight from the tap. Now, we just have to tell all the other humans in the Capital to do the same."

The heavy weight of panic and despondency eased under the realization that they were in the midst of the final push to undo the horror that her father had nearly unleashed on their people.

"Right," she said. "You're right. We have to do this. *I* have to do this."

The alternative—to have gone through all this pain and heartache for *nothing*—was too awful to contemplate.

"You said there was a statement," she said. "Can I see it?"

"Of course." Ash moved back to the console, still favoring just about every muscle in his body, and picked up a padd. He handed it to Skye, who read it over carefully.

"Okay. Okay, I can do this." She looked up at him. "How long to get things set up? And how long will we have before the Regime tracks the signal and shows up at the door?"

Ash looked offended. "The Regime? You obviously still doubt my talents as a tech-worm and hacker. I have no intention of leaving them anything to track."

Skye tried not to show her skepticism, but it must have been apparent anyway, because Ash huffed in annoyance. "Fine. I suppose I'll just have to overlook your lack of faith. Anyway, give me a quarter cycle or so to get things up and running. I've got most of it prepped, but there are still a few details to nail down."

———◆———

It was strangely surreal, sitting in the chair by the console that Ash had vacated, staring into the camera pickup, with her lips a centimeter from the microphone. She knew she looked like she'd been through the wars, but Ash had insisted she not try to clean up.

"More impact this way," he'd said. "Trust me."

Now, he stood off to the side. "Live in four… three… two… *one*." A red light flickered on, next to the screen.

She cleared her throat. The padd with the prepared statement lay on the console in front of her, but she had memorized the contents while she waited, and did not consult it.

"Humans of Ilarius," she began. "My name is Skye Chantrell, daughter of Dr. Zarian Chantrell. My father was a prisoner of the Regime. They forced him to create a deadly bio-weapon for use against the human population of the Capital. Before he was killed, though, he secretly developed an antidote to that weapon, as well.

"My comrades and I have introduced that antidote into the public water supply. Over the coming day, it will spread through the system. Drinking it will protect you from the effects of the weapon. I have tested this personally and can confirm it. To speed the antidote's distribution, please turn on every faucet and water hydrant that you can access, and keep them on.

"Ignore any official Regime announcements about contamination of the water supply—these warnings are untrue, and seek only to minimize the number of humans who are protected against the weapon's effects. Tell everyone you know to drink tap water frequently over the coming days, as the attack is thought to be imminent. Make sure that children, the elderly, and people who may be isolated from outside news drink the water as well.

"The Regime has declared open and deadly warfare on humanity, but we are not without hope, nor without allies. It is time to rise up and fight back against a Premiere with no legitimacy, and no morality.

"Arm yourselves. Organize. Stay strong!"

This was the end of the prepared statement, but the flash of an idea had come to Skye as she was speaking, and she continued.

"Finally, I have a heartfelt plea, from one who has already lost nearly everything to the Regime. Even now, my comrades are struggling to hold the water treatment plant against government forces seeking to shut it down before the antidote can make its way through the system in great enough concentration to be effective.

"If you can get to the plant and help defend it, do so. Block the roads. Fight back. Use the power of numbers against them. Show the Premiere that we will not lie down like sheep at the slaughter. My friends are dying. The man I love... is dying. *Please*. Don't let their deaths be in vain."

The last few words were a hoarse whisper. She cut off the transmission with the flick of a switch, and let her aching head fall into her hands.

"Brilliant," Ash said from beside her. "I should have thought of that, and I didn't. That was *brilliant*, Skye."

His hand closed on her shoulder, and she let the tears fall for a few seconds, unable to hold them back. Ash stepped close enough to pull her against his side while she shivered through the belated re-action. As appreciative as she was not to be alone with her grief and fear, all she could think was how much she wished it was Hunter holding her, instead.

✦

The next three cycles were the longest of Skye's life. Ash had recorded her broadcast, and spent the first cycle releasing it on every hypernet and media site he could hack into. Afterward, he sent a couple of private messages and went out alone for long enough that Skye was starting to seriously worry. He came back just as she was trying to decide what to do if he *didn't*—apologetic, with a small, brown-wrapped package in his hand.

"Sorry about that," he said. "Just when I think all of the optimism has been wrung out of me, it rears its head at the *most* inappropriate of times."

He unwrapped the paper, revealing several shiny little injectors, which he pocketed.

"Neurotonin?" she asked, feeling a surge of bitterness at the reminder of Kade, and his fucking addiction that had probably cost Hunter his life.

"Just in case," Ash said. He turned to the console and pulled up a newsfeed. It was surprisingly free of any news about the water treatment plant, and he frowned. "Looks like a news blackout. We're not far from the plant here, and I can tell you it's getting pretty crazy outside."

He switched the feed over to a low-quality video apparently being taken with a shaky hand-cam. It showed a rowdy mob of demonstrators chanting anti-government slogans.

"Underground news site,' he explained. "Damn, Skye—I think you really started something."

The camera tilted, revealing the distinctive industrial-looking complex housing the water plant, and Skye caught her breath. A stun grenade flashed somewhere in the crowd, sending people scrambling as others fell. Occasional blaster fire whizzed through the shot, followed by screams as the camera wavered crazily.

There was a roar of anger from the crowd, and it *surged*, pressing forward rather than away. The camera steadied, showing people picking up rocks and chunks of concrete… bottles… *anything* that was to hand, and hurling the makeshift projectiles at the half-seen Regime forces trying to hold them back.

Her heart beat faster. The humans were fighting back.

They sat together, watching the feed in silence, while Ash checked periodically to make sure that the layers of protection hiding their transmissions from Regime monitoring were holding.

She was so focused on what was happening on the screen that the flurry of knocks at the door nearly made her jump out of her skin. Ash had the phase rifle pointed at the door before she could blink.

"Get under cover," he said.

Her eyes flew around the room until they settled on the heavy rack of shelves holding the transmission equipment, and she darted behind it.

It's Ryder," came a muffled voice from outside. "Don't blow my head off, Ash."

Ash let out a huge breath, but didn't lower the rifle until the door opened and revealed Ryder, alone, with coppery orange blood dripping down her face.

"I've got wounded incoming," she snapped. "Get me some lights for the stairwell and show me where the medical supplies are stashed."

TWENTY

Skye hesitantly emerged from her hiding place, trying not to let hope surge prematurely. "Wounded?" she asked.

"That's what I said." Ryder sounded at the end of her tether, and Skye tamped down the flood of questions that wanted to rise.

Ash was already up and heading out the door. "This way." He paused at an open breaker box and flipped a couple of switches, presumably to send power to the stairwell lights.

Skye tagged along, her heart pounding like a drum as Ash led Ryder to another unmarked door and palmed the lockpad. The room beyond was as dingy as the rest of the place seemed to be, but there were three cots set up, along with shelves of dusty, vaguely medical-looking tech.

"Charming," Ryder said, but she grabbed a large emergency kit and slung it over her shoulder before hurrying back out.

"Talk to us, Ryder," Ash said, and Skye silently thanked him for saying what she was thinking. She knew Ryder was far less likely to bite Ash's head off than hers, and she was about five seconds from exploding if she didn't get some *answers*.

Ryder threw open the door to the stairwell and started jogging down the first flight. Skye and Ash followed.

"It's a complete clusterfuck out there," Ryder said, not slowing. "Rioters in the streets, attacking the Regime security forces from all sides. No way are they going to be able to get equipment in and shut off that valve before it's too late. So I made an executive decision to get us out of there while the getting was good."

"Casualties?" Ash prompted, and Skye held her breath.

"I brought Hunter with me. He's touch and go. Pax took a shot to the leg, and Draven's arm is dislocated. Kade's down for the count—we had to stun him when he really started to lose his shit from the withdrawal symptoms. Pax is following with him, a few minutes behind me, and then Draven will vape the transporter's control unit so no one can use it to track us here. He'll have to make his way back by alternate means."

During the rundown of injuries, Skye noticed that she had conspicuously failed to mention the gash in her own forehead.

"Okay, no offense, but that's a horrible plan," Ash said, his voice tight. "Draven's injured, and he's a lone Vithii in the middle of a human riot."

Ryder shrugged, and shouldered through the door to the dimly lit basement. "I'm open to alternatives," she said.

"I'll transport out to his position right after Pax arrives, and switch places with him. After I destroy the control unit, I can disappear into the crowd and sneak back here, no problem," Ash told her. He handed her the pack of injectors he'd pocketed earlier. "Here, you'll need these for Kade."

"Yeah, all right," she said. "Thanks. Now, just help me get Hunter off the fucking pad before the others try to transport on top of him, and we end up with a real mess."

Skye's breath caught as she took in the crumpled form lying on the receiving pad. All three of them hurried forward. Ryder took Hunter's shoulders, and she and Ash each took a leg, lifting him as carefully as they could and moving him off the pad. Ryder moved to check his pulse, and Skye's own heart stuttered as the medic cursed under her breath.

"Stubborn bastard," Ryder muttered, and rummaged in the emergency kit for what Skye recognized with a jolt as a portable cardiac defib/pacemaker unit. The medic ripped open Hunter's borrowed uniform shirt and slapped the unit in place. It whined, and a moment later, Hunter's body arched.

The transport unit glowed next to them, a vortex of sparkles resolving into two more figures, one standing and one prone. Pax wavered on his feet for a bare instant before steadying himself.

"That's unpleasant," observed the cyborg, who had a bloody chunk blown out of one massive thigh.

"Clear the pad," Ash said. "I'm transporting over to switch places with Draven." He moved swiftly to the control unit that would allow them to transport out as well as in. Skye hadn't even noticed it sitting there earlier, when Kade had first dragged her here.

Pax nodded his understanding and bent to lift Kade's limp form into a fireman's carry.

Ryder spared Ash a quick glance. "Be prepared to lose your stomach contents, *leetha*. Pax isn't kidding about the ride quality."

Ash hopped on the pad, dropping into a defensive crouch, weapon drawn. "Just as well I skipped lunch, then," he said, and disappeared into a swirl of light.

Draven appeared in his place a moment or two later. He leaned over, gagging a couple of times before he forced his body's reflexes under control. "*Shit*," he said. "Let's... *ugh*... never do this again, all right?"

"Quit moaning," Ryder said without compassion. She had moved from Hunter's side long enough to press one of the neurotonin injectors to Kade's neck, but now she crouched next to Hunter again, across from Skye. "Right, he's about as stable as he's going to be with nearly half his blood volume missing. Pax, can you carry them both?"

"Not with this muscle damage."

"Fine. The three of us will get him upstairs somehow." Ryder checked the cardiac unit one more time and gestured to Draven. "You get the heavy end."

Draven only nodded, and crouched to loop his good arm around Hunter's chest. Skye's stomach churned at the horrible way Hunter's limbs flopped, like a broken doll's. She and Ryder lifted his legs, and the ragtag crew made their way into the cramped stairwell and began the tortuous climb to the upper level.

Skye clutched Hunter's left leg below the knee, trying to will him to hold on. Her own legs were like rubber, but she would have given the last iota of strength in her body—and then some—to get him upstairs to the medical equipment that might yet save his life.

Somehow, they made it. No sooner had they placed their burden on the cot than Ryder rounded on her and Draven. "Out. Both of you. Draven, I'll deal with that arm later."

Skye drew breath to argue. "But—" was all she managed before Draven gently herded her out the door, which closed behind them with an air of finality. She slapped a palm against the peeling paint, feeling suddenly weak.

"Their chances are better if Ryder and Pax aren't distracted," Draven said from behind her. She looked around at him, taking in for the first time how pale and gray his normally copper complexion looked, with beads of sweat on his heavy brow.

"You're in pain," she said stupidly. Of *course* he was in pain, with his left arm dangling limply from its socket.

"It'll keep," Draven said. "Though a place to sit down and some fluids would probably be a good plan right now. Need to keep my strength up enough to rip Ash a new asshole, assuming he makes it back in one piece. The shithead showed up just as I was about to vape the control unit. He told me Ryder needed me *right away, mate*—"

He delivered the last three words in a fair approximation of Ash's Old Earth British accent.

"—and then he practically shoved me onto the pad. Since Ryder obviously *doesn't* need me right away, I figure it was just his martyr complex rearing its head, as per fucking usual."

"He thought it would be easier for a human to blend in with the crowd and get back here on foot," she said. After a last, longing look at the closed door, she turned to him. "Come on. You can sit down and rest in the room where Ash has the transmission equipment set up. I'll find you some food and drink. Can I... help with your arm somehow?"

He shook his head. "Not sure you're strong enough to pop it back in. Thanks for the offer, though."

When she had him settled with a can of tepid Vitharan *edelveen* to drink, she paced restlessly around the room, unable to settle as worry pricked her thoughts like sharp spines.

"So," Draven said eventually, breaking the silence. "You and Hunter, huh?"

She stopped staring at the shelf of incomprehensible tech in front of her. "Yeah," she said heavily. "Me and Hunter. Right up until Kade got him shot because he thought, at some point in the past, that it would be cute to dick around with neurotonin. Never mind that his brain chemistry would be whacked for the rest of his miserable fucking life, and that someone he supposedly considered a friend might *die* because of it—"

"Hey." Draven's voice cut through her rising hysteria. "You're upset. I get it. But you don't know shit about Kade."

She whirled, suddenly spoiling for a fight if it meant she might not have to think about Hunter struggling for his life a few rooms over. "I know enough! He's a fucking *junkie*, and now Hunter might *die*!"

Draven's eyes narrowed. "I'm gonna let that pass, because you're not thinking straight. Also because I'm not as ready to give up on Hunter as you seem to be, and he'd have my intestines for hosepipes if I so much as looked at you wrong. But you listen, and you listen *good*.

"Kade's family was prominent in the Opposition movement ten years ago. They're all dead now. All except him. He was thrown in prison on trumped up charges, instead of being executed. When he started making too much of a stir from the inside with legal challenges and the like, they needed something to make him easier to handle. More *compliant*, like.

"So they started dosing him with neurotonin. Such high doses that he was basically a vegetable. He's lucky they didn't kill him, or put him in a permanent coma. As it was, it took him years to regain full function. And, of course, he'll be dependent on neurotonin for the rest of his life, such as it's likely to be. So don't you fucking talk trash about him when he's not here to defend himself. Because *you. Don't. Know. Shit.*"

The fight went out of her as quickly as it had come. She dropped into the dusty chair in the corner and let her face fall into her hands.

"Prophets. Draven… I'm sorry." She pressed the heels of her hands against her gritty eyes until she saw stars. "Damn it all to hell. I just… need someone to blame, you know?"

"Blame the Regime, in that case. I know I do." Draven's voice still sounded hard, but not as hard as before.

"Yeah," she sighed. "Okay. That sounds like a plan I can get behind."

<hr>

It was two cycles later when Ash trailed back in, sporting a handful of new bruises and scrapes on top of the old ones. Skye wouldn't be able to relax until she heard good news from Ryder, but at least one of her worries fell away on seeing him still mostly in one piece.

"How are the others?" he asked immediately.

"No word yet from Ryder and Pax," Draven said. "They're still in there working on Hunter. Kade got his dose, but there's no telling if it was in time."

"Damn," Ash said.

"They'll be all right," Skye said. She was currently riding the desperately optimistic leg of the emotional rollercoaster she'd been on since they got back, but even she could hear the breakable quality of her voice.

"Of course they will. You know how stubborn those two are," Draven said, with more certainty. "Now. While we're waiting, help me get this blasted shoulder back in its socket so I can kick your fucking ass."

"If you need your arm for kicking, I think that means you're doing it wrong." Ash said, though the sniping was half-hearted. "Come here, then."

Draven painfully lowered himself to lie face up on the open section of floor in front of the equipment shelves, and Ash knelt next to him, moving like an old man. Ash grasped his injured arm with a degree of care that belied their constant arguing, straightening it slowly out to the side.

"Should probably have got you drunk first," he said, grasping Draven's wrist and planting a booted foot under his armpit for leverage.

"No argument here," Draven managed through gritted teeth as Ash put traction on the limb. Skye winced at the wet popping sound as it slid back into place, and winced again at the string of curses that flowed from Draven's lips as he flopped back on the floor, dripping sweat.

"You're welcome," Ash said dryly.

"Fuck you," Draven retorted.

"Better now?" Ash asked, climbing to his feet with stiff movements.

"… yeah," Draven admitted. "I guess. Might just stay down here for a few minutes, though."

"Knock yourself out." Ash took a deep breath. "So, you two. It might not have been the smoothest of operations, and it might not have been without cost… but it appears we've carried it off. Judging by the chrono, a critical mass of nanobots should have entered the city's water system nearly a cycle ago."

A small jolt of shock rippled through the pall of worry that had been smothering Skye's mind. She blinked and drew a breath. "Wait. You mean—?"

Ash smiled. "The antidote is freely available, and so is the message telling people about it. For a given definition of winning… we won."

"Hoo-fucking-ray," said Draven, not moving from his spot on the floor.

A thought occurred, and Skye looked up at Ash with wide eyes. "Ash, you still haven't taken the antidote. You need to drink the water. We've had the taps up here turned on for the last couple of cycles, but the water pressure is practically non-existent."

Ash nodded. "I don't doubt it, since we basically told more than a third of the population to turn on all their faucets as wide as they'd go. We should both drink frequently over the next day or two. The bots multiply quickly, but there's no way to know exactly when they'll get to any individual part of the system."

He disappeared and returned a short time later with two disposable cups, one of which he handed to her. "Cheers," he said, touching the rims together as if they were drinking pints of beer at the pub.

"Bottoms up," she said, still more than a bit in shock at the realization that somehow they'd *done it*. It was *over*. Feeling shaky, she sat down in the chair again.

Now, if only Ryder would let them know what was happening with Hunter and Kade.

———◆———

It was late afternoon, nearly evening when Pax appeared.

"You can go in," he said, his flat, mechanical voice giving nothing away.

Skye was up and out of the door like a shot, drawn to the little converted medical room as though pulled by a magnet. To her dismay, Hunter was still unconscious, deathly pale and terrifyingly corpse-like. She tore her eyes away from him to look at Ryder with an expression that demanded answers.

"He's still alive," the medic said gruffly. "He's got some of Pax's bots in him, working on the damage. He'll either wake up, or he won't."

Skye wanted to weep at the idea that this horrible uncertainty would drag on… for how long?

"When?" she demanded. "When will he wake up?"

Ryder scowled. "Do I look like a fortune teller?"

"She's just worried," Ash said. "We all are. And, doc, if you've done everything you can do right now, you might want to consider lying down on that third cot for a bit, before you fall down. Someone else can keep watch."

Ryder's scowl deepened. "No time for that. I still need to see to Draven's shoulder."

"I already sorted it," Ash said.

"And if you can't tell that just by looking," Draven added, "then you probably *do* need a nap, Ryder."

Ryder's jaw worked. "Pax, will you be functional for the next couple of cycles?" she asked eventually.

"Yes," said the cyborg. "I'll keep watch and wake you at nineteen hundred."

"Or earlier, if there's any change in either of them."

"Of course."

Skye looked between them. "I'm staying."

Ryder eyeballed her. "Really? I would never have guessed."

She could see a hint of the exhaustion and, yes, *fear* hiding behind Ryder's callous facade. Rather than rise to the bait, she said, "Thank you for helping him, Ryder. For helping *them*. You, too, Pax. And—in case you haven't had a chance to check a chrono recently—you did it. The antidote is in the main water supply. You and the others have saved thousands of people's lives."

Ryder wavered a bit and caught herself on the back of a chair, obviously trying to minimize her lapse. Her eyes closed for a moment.

"That's good," she said.

It was too crowded in the small room with all seven of them crammed inside, so Ash and Draven left, allegedly to pursue either mutual drunkenness, the promised ass-kicking, or some combination of the two. Ryder flopped down on the spare cot, fully dressed, and demonstrated one of the universal talents of the medical profession by falling asleep instantly.

Pax limped over to the chair set up by the medical scanner readout screen and sat, his imposing form not nearly as intimidating to Skye as it had been mere days ago. The gaping crater in his thigh was covered with a simple bandage, but it already seemed smaller than it had been when he first arrived.

Skye looked down at Hunter's face. He was so terribly pale—his eyes underlined by dark bags and his cheeks sunken. Faint frown lines marred his face even in unconsciousness. A sheet was drawn over his chest. She couldn't bring herself to pull it back and look at the wound in his side—so similar to the one that had killed her father.

Instead, she quietly pulled up a chair beside the cot and sank into it, gathering one of his hands into both of hers. It felt cold against her skin, so different from the heat she associated with his touch. She chafed it between her palms, trying to warm it.

"I'm not leaving until you wake up," she told him. "I have to tell you that we did it. We *did* it, Hunter. Maybe the Premiere will still launch the weapon, and maybe the antidote won't save everyone… but we still saved thousands of people. You need to wake up so we can celebrate that together."

She bit her lower lip and chewed on it for a moment. "Also," she whispered, "I intend to collect that kiss. Human-style, just like we agreed. I'm holding you to that. Don't… don't leave me alone,

Hunter. Don't you dare give up on me. Not now. Don't you *dare* give up… on *us*."

She lifted his hand to her lips and pressed a kiss to his knuckles. There was no response.

TWENTY-ONE

Hunter's dreams were strange. Disjointed. There was something terribly important he had to do, he was sure. But he couldn't make himself wake up. His body was *there*, lying on its back on something soft. But he could not control it. Not enough for even the barest flicker of an eyelid.

Also, someone was talking to him, much of the time. The tone was odd. Soft. Female. Human?

For quite a while, he thought that perhaps it was Alex or Muriel. Of course, that would mean he was dead, or dying... which sounded about right. Otherwise, he'd be able to open his eyes, surely?

But, no.

He knew the memory of his mothers' voices as well as he knew his own. And he knew this voice, too—but it did not belong to either of them. This voice was... it was...

A jolt made his heart stutter, the first real connection between his mind and body since this strange, dreamy half-life had started.

Skye!

The voice was Skye's. His little human sparrow, with the golden hair and the summer-blue eyes, whom he should not have let himself love because of the danger it put her in. She sounded... *not right*. Why did she sound like that? Was she hurt, or—

The firefight. The water treatment plant. The antidote—

Everything came flooding back. Panic at the idea that Skye and the others might have come to harm while he was unconscious galvanized him. But... wait. He'd sent her away.

Hadn't he?

He'd *meant* to, certainly. A terrible fear gripped him. What if he'd lost consciousness before he could, and had only dreamed that part? Her voice sounded like she was in pain—

His heart pounded, and his breathing grew faster. The movement of his chest sparked burning agony along his side. That was good, though. That was the final connection to his body that he needed.

Other voices were approaching, murky but familiar. With a mighty effort, he blinked open gritty eyes. A confusing blur greeted him. He still couldn't tell where he was.

"Hunter?" A new note entered Skye's voice, though it was still as if he was hearing her through a tunnel.

Other voices wavered in and out. Familiar voices, though he couldn't follow the words. His lips parted as he tried to speak, but only a choked groan emerged.

"Hunter!" Skye called again. "Hunter, if you can understand us, blink your eyes once. Come on... come on, *please*—"

Hunter let his eyelids fall closed. Somehow, despite an effort of will, he couldn't find the strength to open them again.

More time passed. When he next woke, it wasn't because of the voice speaking to him. It was because that voice had gone silent.

Breathing was not quite such an agony this time, though there was a deeply unpleasant pulling sensation in his side where there had been burning pain before. His eyelids opened more easily, and after a few blinks, the ceiling of a dimly lit room came into focus.

Something was restraining his right hand. He rolled his head to that side, letting gravity do most of the work. Skye was asleep in a chair next to him, her upper body slumped awkwardly on the edge of the bed. Both her hands were clutching his, holding it against her cheek as she slumbered.

She looked horrible.

"Decided to join us again?" said a familiar voice, pitched low, but no less acerbic for it. *Ryder.* "Do try to stick around a bit longer this time, if it's not too much trouble."

A brief smile touched his lips at her scathing tone. She must have been really worried to have achieved such a level of bedside abrasiveness. The smile disappeared as, once again, his memory started to fill in the blanks. With effort, he rolled his head to the other side so he could meet Ryder's eyes.

She must have seen the question on his face.

"All good news, don't worry. Well… *mostly* good news, at any rate," she said. "First things first, though. Drink. Only a sip or two, mind you." A practiced hand lifted his head and guided his lips to a straw. He sipped and swallowed cool water that felt like paradise as it trickled down his parched throat.

"Can you speak?" Ryder asked.

His tongue felt about twice as big as he thought it should, but he managed to croak, "Yes."

"All right. In that case, I'm going to wake sleeping beauty over there. Do us all a favor and don't pass out on her again without saying something reassuring first."

A frown settled over Hunter's features as he looked back at Skye. Even in the low light, he could see the dark circles under her eyes and the bloodless, pale slash of her mouth. Ryder crossed to the other side of the cot and shook Skye's shoulder. She jerked awake with a gasp. He tried to squeeze her hands, but it felt like his fingers barely twitched.

It was enough. She stared at their joined hands, and then her eyes flew to his face, her lips parting.

"He's awake," Ryder said. "Properly, this time. Don't wear him out or jar his side."

"Hunter?" Skye asked, in a tiny voice.

"I'm here, sparrow." Despite his best efforts, the words were still only a hoarse whisper. "It's all right."

Suddenly, her hands were no longer holding his, but instead, were touching his face… his hair… his neck…

"Oh, gods… *Hunter*," she breathed, and then her lips were on his—a human kiss.

His arm seemed to weigh ten times what it should have, but that didn't stop him from lifting it to encircle her. The movement was clumsy, but it didn't matter—he *needed* to have her safe in his embrace. Details were unimportant.

He felt the first hitch of a sob rise through her chest and emerge as a warm puff of air against his lips. She clutched the bare skin of his shoulders and buried her face against his neck, crying.

Hunter held her, and looked up at Ryder a bit helplessly.

"It's just relief, and probably delayed reaction to trauma," Ryder said. "I'll give you a few minutes and get the others so we can give you a full report."

"The others?" he prompted.

"All alive," she confirmed. "Even Kade. Though he's spent the last couple of days wishing he wasn't, I suspect."

Hunter relaxed, and turned his full attention back to Skye, still sniffling in his embrace and holding him as if she was afraid he'd disappear like smoke.

"She never left your side, you know," Ryder said softly. "The Premiere unleashed the bio-weapon the morning after we released the antidote. It protected her and Ash from the full effects, but they were still sick as dogs for a while. She wouldn't leave you, though. Not even when she was repeatedly puking her guts out."

With that, Ryder turned and left, presumably to tell the others he was awake. An unaccustomed wash of emotion pulled at his chest and gut. "Oh, Skye," he murmured.

"I couldn't leave you alone in the dark," she said against his skin. "So I stayed, and talked to you. About anything. About everything. I didn't know if you could hear me, but—"

"I heard you," he said.

She nodded against his shoulder. "*Good.*"

The door swung open, revealing all of the others except Ash. Hunter's eyes sought Kade, who was moving like an old, old man, stoop-shouldered, with a visible tremor in his hands.

"Stop staring, *tei'laal*," Kade said. "At least I look better than you."

Something settled in Hunter's chest at Kade's words, but he still needed to speak. "You kept your vow to me, but I broke mine to you."

Kade dropped into a chair near the door and waved the words off impatiently. "I got you shot in the process, so I think we're more than even," he said.

To Hunter's surprise, Skye spoke up before he could, straightening away from him and reclaiming his hand again.

"That's bull, Kade," she said. "You said yourself that all the metal pipes in the treatment plant were playing havoc with the scanner. Chances are, you didn't see the sniper move into position because it was a single person, quite a distance away, and he was right in the middle of all that metal and flowing water. Besides, you *did* spot him before it was too late. If you want to blame someone, blame Hunter for being a self-sacrificing *idiot*."

"Hunter's *always* been a self-sacrificing idiot," Draven put in from where he was lounging against the wall.

"Agreed," Pax said, deadpan as always.

"Yup," Ryder chimed in.

"Where's Ash?" Hunter asked gruffly, because it was an important question, and *not* because it would change the subject.

"Back at his place, trying not to arouse suspicion, and playing at normalcy," Kade said. "As much as anyone can, under the circumstances."

Hunter had grasped the bare outline of events, but a lot had obviously happened while he was out of commission. "And… what *are* the circumstances?"

Skye said, "The others held the position around the shutoff valve while Ash and I sent out a city-wide transmission over hijacked vid channels. We called for any humans in the area to block the roads and attack the Regime forces that were trying to get into the plant. The demonstrations and rioting spread across the city, and once the antidote was safely loose in the water supply, the others transported back here."

"At which point," Kade added, "A certain human who was already on my shit list vaped a very expensive matter transport control unit, after I distinctly said I didn't want it damaged."

Ryder glared at him. "Yeah. Because it would have been *so* much better to leave it there and have Regime goons transport into the basement after us."

Kade glared back. "It's a *matter transport unit.* You could have put it on the fucking pad and used the other *matter transport unit* to beam it back here to the basement. It's not fucking *brain surgery.*"

"I have actually *done* brain surgery, you realize," Ryder said, unimpressed.

"C'mon, Kade," said Draven. "You've at least gotta give Ash points for scoring you some neurotonin while they were waiting. Otherwise, you'd've been worm food."

Kade subsided. "Yeah. Well. That's why I haven't pummeled him yet."

"That, and the fact that he could probably wipe the floor with you right now, the state you're in," Pax observed.

"*Anyway*," Skye said. "That was four days ago. The Capital has pretty much been in chaos. The Premiere released the bio-weapon over the city the following morning. A lot of people had already gotten the antidote from the water supply. A bunch more started swilling it once they saw that it wasn't a hoax, and an attack really was happening. But… a lot of people are still dying."

Hunter ached at the pain in her voice as she spoke the last words.

"It was never going to be a perfect solution," Pax said. "Some wouldn't believe the threat was real. Some wouldn't have access, or the concentration of antidote wouldn't be high enough in the water they drank. Some would be too weak or old or young to survive even the milder sickness caused by the bio-agent after ingesting the water. It was still a preferable plan to doing nothing."

"I know. We saved thousands of lives, Hunter," Skye said. "But many hundreds have still died. And, thanks to underground media coverage and the hypernet, those deaths are emblazoned for everyone in the Seven Systems to see. There's outrage, and it's growing. The Premiere was a fool to use the weapon after so many people were already protected from its effects."

"There will be civil war soon," Pax predicted. "Though it remains to be seen precisely where the battle lines will fall."

Ryder had been watching Hunter carefully throughout.

"Right," she said. "That's enough for now. Hunter, all you need to focus on is this—the building is still secure for the moment, and you're weak as an infant. We'll be moving to a new safehouse on the outskirts of the city in a couple of days. In the mean time, you and your human shadow both need to rest. That goes for you, too, Kade. I don't want to see any of you doing anything more strenuous than sleeping, eating, and taking a shit until then."

"Yes, *ma'am*," Kade said, sarcasm heavy in his voice as he snapped off a jaunty salute with one unsteady hand. "I'll just be down the hall, in that case, so I don't have to try to sleep through these two whispering sweet nothings to each other. I've lost enough brain cells over the last few days as it is."

"Sleep well, *tei'laal*," Hunter said, unperturbed. Kade only grunted and raised a careless hand as he left the room.

"It's good to see you awake, boss," Draven said. "We'll keep an eye on things while you recover."

"Thank you." Hunter met their eyes in turn. "All of you. I've done nothing to deserve your continued loyalty, but I value it greatly, all the same."

"As long as you value it enough to avoid getting shot through the liver in the future," Ryder said, gruff. "At the rate he's been giving them away, Pax isn't going to have enough bots left to maintain his own systems."

Pax hadn't moved from his place across the room, but now he shot Ryder a dark look. "Don't employ hyperbole. It's good to see them going toward something positive after what they've been used for in the past."

Ryder shrugged. "They definitely have their uses. Now, everyone out. Hunter's been awake long enough."

Skye's grip on his hand tightened. "I'm not leaving."

Ryder rolled her eyes. "Yeah, no kidding. I think we all got that part. Now get some sleep. *In a bed*."

The others left, and Skye sagged, obviously exhausted beyond endurance.

"Ryder's right," Hunter told her. "Sleep now. In a bed."

She looked at him with an expression of longing he couldn't have resisted if he'd tried. "She... didn't specify *which* bed, though. Did she?"

He smiled. "No. I suppose she didn't, at that."

The cot was sized for a single Vithii, and Hunter was so weak he couldn't even roll over to give her more space. Space wasn't what either of them wanted, though. Even so, when she was settled on his uninjured side, half draped across his body, he had a hard time believing she could be comfortable. Yet, within moments, her tense muscles relaxed, molding against him, and her breathing evened out, growing slow and deep.

"Love you so much, Hunter," she murmured against his chest. "Please never scare me like that again..."

With that, she was asleep.

He wanted to stay awake for a bit. Feel her sleeping in his embrace. But as if her presence was a drug, the warm weight of her pulled him inexorably down into dreams as well.

A week and a day after the Premiere tried to commit genocide against her people, Skye sat in the modest courtyard of the hundred-year-old building that was their current safehouse. It was too dangerous for her, Hunter, or Pax to go outside—especially in daylight. They were too recognizable, and too wanted.

She'd been pleasantly surprised to discover, however, that the salty tang and cool northerly breeze coming off of the nearby ocean penetrated the little open cloister at the center of the old structure. The slender branches of an ancient *chik'taap* tree protected them from aerial or satellite surveillance, but a smattering of ever shifting, dappled sunlight still made its way to the ground at midday.

It had taken a few days of soaking up Hunter's living, breathing, *recovering* presence before she'd been able to bring herself to leave his side for any length of time. But she was finally to the point where she didn't immediate feel the urge to run back and check *one more time* that he was truly, actually okay.

That morning, she'd been beset by thoughts of Temple, and she'd finally decided to come out and sit alone for a while to brood. She was still mourning her father. She also felt terrible guilt over the knowledge that she'd left her stepmother rotting in a Regime cell... for all that she could never stand the woman.

Temple, though... Temple was a question mark. A gaping hole in her emotions. She didn't know whether to mourn him, fear for him, or feel guilty about him. Ash had smiled kindly at her when she'd brought it up, and promised to look into it. But everyone knew that the Regime's prison system was a black hole—especially for humans.

People went in, but no information got out. Nothing escaped the event horizon beyond vague rumors of the horrors that must surely take place within. She knew it was far more likely her foster brother had been killed while trying to protect her. And maybe that was a mercy, of sorts.

Her bleak thoughts were interrupted by the sound of slow, halting footsteps approaching from behind. She turned to find Hunter limping toward her, leaning heavily on the makeshift cane Ryder had provided him. He was much improved, thanks to a combination of Pax's nanotech knitting his guts back together, and the blood transfusions Ryder had taken from Kade once the other man was far enough along in his own recovery.

"I have to filter out the blasted neurotonin before I can use it," the medic had groused, "but he's the only one here who's a blood-type match."

"That's why it's more than half a joke that they call each other tei'laal," Draven put in, grinning. "It means 'blood brother'."

Hunter should have been dead, but he wasn't. Neither of them was. It was still a bit difficult for her to wrap her brain around that, sometimes.

"Brooding alone, little sparrow?" he asked, his green eyes soft.

She smiled, unable to focus on the horrors of life when he looked at her like that. "You bet. I do all my best brooding in solitude. Don't try to tell me that's a foreign concept to you."

Amusement flickered over his heavy features. "Not at all, no." He sobered and took a deep breath, as if gathering himself for something, and her brow furrowed.

"Is something wrong?" she asked.

"No," he said quickly. "Nothing like that." His throat bobbed. "I... I have a request to make of you. That's all."

His uncharacteristic uncertainty deepened her frown, but she allowed him to reach down and help her rise from the old stone bench where she'd been sitting. He leaned the cane carefully against the seat so he could take both of her hands in his.

"What is it, Hunter?" she asked, looking up at him intently.

"Sorry, I'm not good at this." He cleared his throat. "Skye, of House Chantrell—soul of my soul—I am not complete without you. I humbly ask the honor of your trust. Join with me, that I may be bonded to you and yours, and protect you always."

Skye's lips parted, and a tiny gasp slipped out. Her heart stuttered and skipped a beat before pounding back to life, the sudden rush of blood making her lightheaded. Could this really be happening? Could... they actually *have* this, amidst all the horror and death?

Words fell out of her mouth in a tumble before she realized how they might sound. "But... Hunter... I'm *human*. And you're Vithii. And... how could we even have a ceremony like that? I mean, it's not as though the two of us can run down to the nearest courthouse and petition the magistrate for a cross-species marriage license—"

She saw the light dim in his eyes; saw the barriers coming up, and snapped her jaw shut.

"I… understand, sparrow," he said. "It was inappropriate of me to ask. Forgive my presumption."

TWENTY-TWO

"No," she said quickly, squeezing his hands hard when he started to pull away. "Hunter, no! I'm the one who should ask forgiveness. The answer is yes. Yes, I'll bond with you! But I know nothing about Vithii marriage rituals. I don't even know the proper response I'm supposed to give..." she trailed off and swallowed. "... as you may have gathered, just now."

Hunter let out a breath in obvious relief, and she marveled that *she*, of all people, could apparently have this effect on the most feared man in the Seven Systems. Could reduce a dangerous alien vigilante to a nervous wreck, hanging on her every word.

"The usual response is, *I freely give you my trust, heart of my heart*," he replied, a touch of humor returning to his deep voice. "But, that being said, I'm not in a mood to be picky."

She smiled, a sudden swell of happiness the likes of which she hadn't known for *years* making her chest feel light and open.

"I freely give you my trust, heart of my heart," she said, gazing into his depthless eyes.

His smile was like the sun coming out from behind the clouds.

"Okay," she said, giddy, "I *really* need a kiss right now—human custom or no."

Hunter *laughed*, and she realized with a jolt that she had never *once* heard him do so before. "And I *really* need to mark you now," he shot back. "Vithii custom or no."

The light feeling in her chest overflowed, and Skye surged up, freeing a hand to twist in his loose shirt and drag him down, pressing their lips together. As he had on previous occasions, he let her explore his mouth, remaining largely passive. She knew he still didn't remotely understand human kissing... but that was fine with her.

More than fine. It meant that she would have something to teach him over the course of the rest of their lives—however long or short a time that might be.

When they parted for air, he smiled at her again, lazy and wicked. With both hands, he lifted her right wrist slowly to his lips, never breaking eye contact. Her breathing sped up as he nipped along the tendon until he came to her pulse point.

She would never in a million years have pegged her *wrist* as an erogenous zone, but as he pulled the thin skin between his teeth and sucked a dark bruise to the surface, bright little pinpricks of almost-pain as he worried at her delicate flesh zipped down the length of her spine to settle low in her belly, heavy and liquid.

When he let her skin slip free of his lips and teeth, she looked down at the livid love bite that marked her as his, and shivered.

"Yeah," she said, faintly shaky. "Okay. I'm really starting to warm to the Vithii alternative to kissing."

"I'll remind you of that when you're lying spent and exhausted in my bed on our bonding night, your body covered in my marks." The dark velvet of his voice made the ache in her belly grow deeper.

"You do that," she managed. With considerable difficulty, she dragged her mind out of the delicious filth of the gutter where it was happily wallowing, and back to practicalities. "Seriously, though—how can we have a ceremony? There's really no one we can trust to perform it right now."

"Not true," Hunter said easily. "Pax holds the rank of full Commander in the Ilarian military. He's perfectly qualified to perform formal bondings."

She frowned in shock. "He... *does*? But I thought..."

"That he was a ne'er-do-well gutter rat like the rest of us? Gutter rats don't get cyber-enhancement, sparrow. He served in the military for many years, and was retired with full honors." His voice and expression grew hard. "Right before he was sent to be *decommissioned*. I'll leave it to your imagination what that particular euphemism entails, for a cyborg."

"He escaped before they could kill him," she realized.

"Because his superiors no longer considered him a *useful commodity*. So, he eventually washed up here," Hunter agreed. "Fortunately for all of us, I might add, since both you and I would be dead if it weren't for him, and his generosity with the nano-tech swimming around in his bloodstream."

"You, me, and most of the human population of the capital, you mean," Skye said. "Yes—if he's willing to do it, I'd be honored beyond belief for Pax to perform the ceremony."

"I'll talk to him right away," Hunter said.

The bonding ceremony took place two days later in the same courtyard where Hunter had proposed to her. In the absence of her father and brother, Ash had agreed to give her away in a nod to human custom. For the first time since she had met him, his various bruises and welts were mostly healed. He'd pulled his long black hair back into a ponytail, and was wearing a perfectly tailored black Nehru suit for the occasion, the elegant cut complementing his slender, athletic build.

The others wore mostly dark colors as well, but each had some item of vibrant blue, in the case of the men, and orange, in Ryder's case. Skye had seen the color scheme before in important Vithii ceremonies, though she was unsure of its significance. One of many things she would need to learn.

She'd been dismayed to realize that she still only had her plain black jumpsuit to wear, but Ash had taken care of that for her. He was the one who still had the most freedom to move around in the outside world, and he'd quietly acquired a dress for her.

It was made in a simple, sleeveless, form-fitting style that hugged her body to the knee before flaring out to brush the floor. It fit perfectly, and the cut flattered her tall, rather gawky frame as much as anything could, she thought. The material and color, however, were what made it special. It was a deep shade of burnished copper, made from something silky. The dappled light in the courtyard played over it like sun on rippling water, as though the dress itself were made of liquid metal.

She loved it.

She also loved that she was barefoot for the ceremony, her toes sinking softly into the grass of the courtyard as Ash walked her toward the center, where Hunter and Pax were waiting for her.

She was aware of the others, flanking one side of the path. Of Draven's eyes following her and Ash, a cryptic expression on the Vithii male's normally open face. Of Kade's careful detachment. Of Ryder trying to cover an expression of bitterness and… fear? Skye knew all of them had hidden depths she had yet to plumb. But for now, they were *here*—Hunter's ragtag family, for better or worse, come to support his bonding ceremony.

Most of her attention, however, was reserved for the man waiting for her. Hunter had refused to use his cane during the ceremony. He was barefoot, as she was, wearing dark trousers and a blue silk shirt—open, for the ceremony, to display his heart. His green eyes focused on her to the exclusion of all else as she approached. That gaze—dark and hungry—made her want to grab him and drag him inside *right this instant*. Screw the bonding ritual.

But of course, they weren't actually going to do that.

Pax stood a few steps behind Hunter, implacable as ever; wearing the same dark colors as the others, with a sapphire blue sash slung across his massive chest. Ash led her to stand next to Hunter and took a step to the side, out of the way.

Pax spoke into the expectant silence. "We gather here today to witness the joining of House Chantrell and House Tarthasian in a bonding ceremony. Who here speaks for House Chantrell?"

Ash cleared his throat. "In the absence of those who should so speak—I do. Ash of House Shadow Wing."

Pax nodded. "And what say you, Ash of House Shadow Wing?"

"I say that Skye of House Chantrell agrees freely and joyfully to the union with her intended mate."

Pax's eyes moved to Skye, his metal facial implants glinting in the light. She tore her gaze away from Hunter with difficulty to look at him.

"Is this true, Skye of House Chantrell?" Pax asked.

"It's true," she said. "I agree to the bonding freely and joyfully."

Pax looked to Hunter. "Who speaks for House Tarthasian?"

Kade took a step forward. "In the absence of those who should so speak—I do. Kade of House Shadow Wing."

"And what say you, Kade of House Shadow Wing?"

"I say that Hunter of House Tarthasian vows protection and devotion toward his intended mate—both his own protection, and that of his family of choice, House Shadow Wing. He—and they—do solemnly swear to act in the best interest of House Chantrell for as long as the last member of each House shall live."

A lump formed in Skye's throat.

"Is this true, Hunter of House Tarthasian?" Pax asked.

"On my life, it is true," Hunter said. "I will protect and defend House Chantrell with my last breath, freely and joyfully."

Skye's breath hitched, tears burning behind her eyes. She refused to let them fall.

"So be it," Pax said. "Which House name will you both take, as bondmates?"

They had discussed this earlier, so it was no surprise when Hunter said solemnly, "We choose the name of House Shadow Wing."

Pax inclined his head. "Then present your hands to complete the bonding, Hunter and Skye of House Shadow Wing."

Hunter and Skye held their hands out, palm up. Skye felt a flash of nervousness as Pax drew a small, wicked blade from his sash. The cyborg nicked the heel of Hunter's hand with the knife, and a few beads of copper-orange blood welled up. Skye held her breath as he did the same to her, bringing a couple drops of bright red to the surface. The blade was so sharp that she had barely felt it part her flesh.

"Join hands," Pax ordered, and they laced their fingers together, blood mingling as their palms pressed against each other.

Pax produced a length of blue ribbon and a length of orange ribbon, which he skillfully wound around their joined hands, the two colors weaving together in such a way that the ends would not pull loose.

"You are now bonded," he said. "Accept the blood vows of House Shadow Wing, and celebrate your union before the eyes of the prophets, and the people of Ilarius."

Skye's eyes flew back to Hunter, whose own crinkled at the edges. She could feel the faint sting of the tiny cut on her hand, pressed to his—that same little sharp bite of sensation she'd felt when he marked her wrist after she'd accepted his proposal, making everything feel more real.

One by one, the others were coming up, drawing blades from their clothing and slicing small cuts into their palms, as well. Each of them let a few precious drops of blood fall into the ceremonial crystal bowl set next to where Pax had officiated—a vow to protect the new union against all harm.

She wondered idly where they had gotten the bowl. It was beautiful, and almost certainly an antique. Perhaps it had simply been in the house somewhere, gathering dust for the last few decades.

Ash kissed the knuckles of her free hand before adding a few drops of his red human blood to the bowl. "I'm happy for you, you know," he said, something wistful in his demeanor as his gaze widened to encompass Hunter as well. "Both of you."

"Thank you for giving me away," Skye said softly.

Ash smiled. "It was my honor."

Hunter looked at him intently. "Thank you… for *everything*. Your family is here for you, *leetha*, should you ever have need of us. No matter what."

For a moment, Ash looked… *devastated*. He covered it quickly—once again the debonair charmer—and Skye wondered if she'd truly seen the lost expression.

"Me? Need help? You know I've never found a corner I couldn't wriggle out of," he said. "Still, I'm touched. All this time, Hunter, and I never knew you cared." Ash gave her a quick, brittle grin. "Now, enjoy your wedding night, won't you? You know what they say about Vithii males…"

Hunter frowned, looking between them. "No, I don't. What do they say?"

Ash only laughed, and slipped away. Skye saw Draven's dark eyes follow him from the courtyard, staring after him for a long time after he disappeared back into the house.

Ryder took his place at the bowl, eyeing it with distaste before spilling a few drops of copper blood into it. "Superstitious, unhygienic nonsense," she muttered.

Hunter smiled at her fondly. "And yet, you indulge it."

She stared back at him, deadly serious. "*You,* Hunter. Do a better job than my mate did," she said cryptically, before turning her attention to Skye. "And, *you.* Don't wear him out. He's still not completely recovered."

"We'll be careful," Skye promised. "Thank you, Ryder. We both owe you so much."

Ever the soul of tact and diplomacy, Ryder only grunted and waved off the words. Kade replaced her, the last member of the strange little procession.

Hunter raised an eyebrow. "I think you've let more than enough blood for me over the past few days, *tei'laal.*"

Kade made a scoffing noise and sliced his hand. "Don't be an ass. It's the principle of the thing, as you well know."

Skye took a deep breath. "I owe you an apology, Kade," she said. "Probably several, now that I think about it."

He looked at her for a beat. "Save us both the embarrassment, if you wouldn't mind, and we'll take it as given."

She bit her lip and nodded.

"Are we all right, *tei'laal*?" Hunter asked. "You and I?"

Kade's brows drew together. "When have you and I ever *not* been all right?" He took a breath and let it out. "Your timing may suck like a black hole, but I don't begrudge you the happiness I can never have. Now, get out of here, both of you. Go fuck like rabbits, preferably somewhere that I don't have to hear it."

When he had gone, Hunter looked down at her, his eyes going soft and dark. "Even considering the source, little sparrow, some advice is worth following without question."

Skye couldn't have stopped the slow smile that spread across her face if she'd tried. "Which advice is that?" she asked innocently. "The *don't wear you out* advice, or the *fuck like rabbits* advice?"

"Come inside, and I'll be happy to clarify," he shot back.

Her grin turned feral. "Oh, I think you're the one who'll be *coming inside*," she said, drawing a pained groan from him.

"Just for *that*..." he said, and scooped her up over his shoulder, holding her as if she weighed nothing, despite his recent injuries.

She squealed and clung to him, their fingers still tangled where their hands were bound together by the ribbons. Giddiness flooded through her, and erupted into peals of helpless laughter as he hauled her into the depths of the old house, toward their bedroom.

Much later, she lay curled on her side in a sweaty, exhausted heap, just as he had warned earlier—sated, deliciously sore, and covered with his marks. Hunter lay on his uninjured side, spooning her from behind, his lips playing over the love bite he'd left at the juncture of her neck and shoulder as he'd entered her from behind.

The shivery feeling as he worried at the tender mark flowed down her spine to where they were still joined together, and her inner walls fluttered around the thick heat of his knot. Needing to see him, she craned around to look over her shoulder.

He abandoned his efforts on her neck and shoulder in favor of propping himself up on an elbow so he could offer her a human kiss. The angle was awkward and he was still unpracticed, but the metaphorical light bulb had finally flickered into life above his head earlier, when he'd realized that nipping, nibbling, and sucking on her lower lip while kissing was not only tolerated, but encouraged.

The last tiny bit of tension flowed from her body as his full lips slid against hers, and he smiled down at her as he pulled away and tucked her more fully against his firm-muscled body.

"*Now*, you finally begin to feel the effects of the coital trance, as a female should," he teased. "Obviously, I just wasn't patient enough before."

"Mmm..." she managed, melting into a happy puddle in his arms.

She felt his answering rumble of amusement travel from his body to hers, where they were pressed together.

"Human females are *exhausting*," he murmured, in between nips as he returned his single-minded focus to the nape of her neck.

"You love it," she said with complete certainty, utterly relaxed as new waves of pleasure washed through her. When Hunter had first explained the coital trance to her, she'd thought Vithii women must be missing out on quite a bit during sex with their impressively endowed men. Now, she was starting to think they might be onto something, after all.

The feeling of absolute safety and tranquility made it easier to think about the future, and she asked, "What will we do now, Hunter?"

He lifted a hand to stroke the hair away from her face, smoothing it back in a slow, soothing caress.

"We will love each other, little sparrow. With all our hearts," he said. His knuckles brushed her cheek tenderly. "We will look after our friends—our *family*—and they will look after us. Together, we will fight for what is right. What else could we possibly do?"

Skye nodded. What indeed? The future was unwritten. It would be up to them to shape it into what it needed to be.

EPILOGUE

The cells in the underbelly of the Regime's compound were dark and cold. There were no comforts here. No cots. No pillows or blankets. Just a cramped, bare room with metal bars and a small, stinking hole in the plasticrete floor for waste.

Even here, though, news traveled.

Heavy footsteps echoed down the corridor beyond the bars—guards approaching. Moans and whimpers of terror emerged from other cells as the Vithii men stopped in front of a barred door two cells down.

"Prisoner two-four-one-three-six," barked one of the guards. "Face the back wall and present your hands for manacles."

Sobs of fear echoed along the cellblock as the unlucky human was chained, muzzled, and dragged from her cell. Temple closed his eyes and pressed his naked back harder into the corner, trying not to let it get to him. The bruises from his last beating ached as the cold from the walls leached into his flesh.

He knew where they were taking her, of course. And he knew that she wouldn't be coming back. Whispers had been making the rounds for days now—the Premiere had tried to kill the humans in the Capital with a bio-weapon, but it hadn't worked as intended. The first time he'd heard the news, Temple had to bite his cheek until it bled to avoid showing any overt reaction.

Shortly afterward, half of the prisoners in his block had been given bottled water instead of the bucket of lukewarm tap water they'd been accustomed to receiving every morning. The next day, the guards started taking random prisoners away, and only the ones who'd drunk from the buckets came back. They were weak and sick, but they were alive.

The ones who'd been given bottled water—like the woman they'd taken just now—didn't return. The Vithii were experimenting on them, said the survivors. Exposing them to the bio-agent. Using them as disposable lab rats.

Which meant... that Skye had made it out. Somehow, his foster sister had escaped and saved the humans in the city from genocide. Was she still alive? He couldn't be sure.

Sometimes, he liked to pretend that she was; that she had found a safe haven somewhere, as unlikely as that seemed, and was even now plotting to free him from the Regime's hands in some crazy rescue like you might see in a cheap holodrama. Other times, that kind of hope was too painful, and he pictured her going out in a blaze of glory, a sneer of victory twisting her features as she fell, cut down cleanly by a stray blaster beam. Secure in the knowledge that she had saved the day.

Neither option seemed terribly likely.

One thing Temple was quite sure of, though. His captors knew exactly who he was, and how they might use him for leverage if Skye *was* still alive. That knowledge would almost certainly prevent him from being used as a lab experiment by the psychos up in Weapons Research, in the short run.

But in the long run, it was bad, *bad* news. Both for him, and for Skye.

finis

The *Love and War* series continues with Book 2: *Antigen.*

To discover more books by this author, visit www.rasteffan.com